ANN CRAMER

WISHING *Martha* A *Mary* CHRISTMAS

Celebrating Christmas in your heart as well as under your tree

Published by hope*books
2217 Matthews Township Pkwy
Suite D302
Matthews, NC 28105
www.hopebooks.com

hope*books is a division of hope*media

Printed in the United States of America

First paperback edition.
Paperback ISBN: 979-8-89185-296-9
Hardcover ISBN: 979-8-89185-297-6
Ebook ISBN: 979-8-89185-298-3
Library of Congress Number: 2025945397

For Jesus

Who lovingly wrote these words on my heart and

Who's been writing on my heart all along

Happy Birthday

pa rum pum pum pum

Table of Contents

It's Christmas, Prepare for Impact

I slammed on the brakes as a horrible screech echoed through the car. I had hit the brick wall at the edge of our driveway. That wall had always been a menace, sitting there just waiting for me to misjudge by an inch. But tonight, I had more than misjudged. I was practically on top of it. Silence filled the car, except for the now-annoying sound of Jingle Bells on the radio. I glanced in the rearview mirror. Three sets of wide eyes, Ashley's, Bo's, and Mac's, all stared right back at me. Much like little judges, all ready to declare me guilty. In their version of events, of course, I had almost killed them.

You see, it all began, as most December plans do, with the ambitious belief that this Christmas season was going to be perfect. Towards that goal, we scheduled an outing to our local mall that sponsored a Christmas carousel, which our kids absolutely loved. So we planned an evening of dinner and a few spins on the merry-go-round to get our season started. By 5:00 P.M., the kids and I were fully committed and decked out in our finest Christmas sweaters (or sweatshirts, because it was, after all, the mid-'90s, and fashion was just so awful). We were dressed, excited, and getting very hungry. And that's when the mood started to shift.

The phone rang. Bob. My husband. A young attorney. He was delayed. More time passed. Hunger and restlessness grew. The phone rang again. Not good news. Moods shifted. Joy shifted. Time passed. Further detained. Yet another call. Even more delayed.

At this point, my mood had plunged to anger that our first holiday outing was being sabotaged. The children had become fussy, complete with whining, flopping onto furniture, and making dramatic claims about imminent starvation. So, in a bold act to heroically save our perfect Christmas, I did what any determined holiday mom would do. I loaded them into the car, started the Christmas music, and sort of aggressively floored it out of the driveway. Little did I know that the wall, yes, that wall, was also about to attempt to steal my holiday spirit. So there we were, wedged against the wall so tightly that I wasn't sure if I should pull forward or stay in reverse. But, in the spirit of Christmas marital stress, I was mighty sure of one thing: this was definitely my husband's fault.

Joy to the world, it was Christmas again, and we were just getting started...

Oh Come All Ye Frazzled

I love beginnings! There's something exhilarating about standing on the first tee in golf or feeling the anticipation of a coin toss before your team's big game. Remember the feeling of a new school year, with all your new supplies in tow and walking into your classroom on the first day? It's a clean slate and a fresh start. Each fall at the beach, we watch as fishing boats head out early on Saturday mornings. Dozens of them, 60 or 70, troll for bait, making their final preparations before each one sets off to their secret lucky spot, convinced the prize fish is waiting there. They're fresh, rested, and ready to go. Both their expectations and excitement are buoyed by their readiness for the task ahead. But being game-ready takes time, practice, and intentional effort. No one, successful at least, just arrives and wins without a plan and some preparation.

The Lord is showing me that I need to approach Christmas like game time, ready and prepared. That means not only tackling all the seasonal to-dos early, but also having a plan to prioritize my own spiritual health and growth amidst all the holiday distractions. Like Martha in Luke's gospel, it's not what we are busy doing that is wrong. It's just that seeking our to-do list first and foremost will not sustain us spiritually. If our focus is only on the busy, we'll end up exhausted rather than fulfilled. Isn't joy what we want for ourselves? And isn't joy what we want to ultimately offer our friends and families at Christmas? We must have a plan that sustains our own joy if we are to have any to spread to others.

Christmas should be a time when we draw closer to the Lord. After all, we're celebrating His birthday! We sing about God's greatest gift to the world, how Jesus came to save us from sin, and how He showed us a new way to live. We rejoice in the depth of God's love, sending His only Son for us. And yet, we fit all of this right alongside everything else on our holiday to-do list, giving it no more priority than wrapping presents or planning meals. We get caught in a rhythm of checking off tasks, pushing forward just to make it to Christmas morning. We make Jesus an accessory for the season instead of the reason for the season. There's little time to pause, let alone intentionally slow down and re-evaluate our priorities. When you're constantly feeling behind, adding one more thing, even something sacred, feels impossible.

It was as I reflected on my own exhaustion and frustration, fueled by this state of perpetual busyness, that the Lord put this book on my heart. The last thing I wanted to do, though, was give you or me another thing to do at Christmas. How does an already overly busy person find time to read a book, evaluate their priorities, and perhaps even change course? As I talked to other women about this issue, I realized that it might be best to offer this book beginning in October, when all the holiday catalogs are arriving, so it can be used as a motivator to plan for your spiritual Christmas early, just like we plan ahead for our cultural celebration.

So maybe this year, we don't just add time with Jesus to the list. Perhaps we start there. Maybe He's intended to be our resting place during all the chaos. I pray that the following pages will bless you and encourage you to prepare early, not just your shopping and decorating, but spiritually as well. If we don't go into Advent spiritually ready, we will not be able to sustain our joy through Christmas. It's just too easy to be distracted and get off our path. I've kept each section short, making the book easy to pick up whenever you can steal a quiet moment. You'll find personal reflection prompts at the end of each section. My hope is that these pages give you space to pause, reflect, and reset. Chaos, fatigue, and spiritual burnout are the results of a worldly Christmas and not at all what Jesus desires for us.

But pausing is hard. The season is just such a whirlwind, physically and mentally draining, as it is full of contradictions and choices! Have you ever thought of how many decisions you make in December? From the big ones, like where to spend Christmas morning. To the tiny ones, like which wrapping paper to use or what kind of cookies to bake. We're constantly facing options. There are so many choices of how to do things and resources available to us now that we are continually confronted with decisions. But the Christmas you and I long for, the one that brings peace, meaning, and joy, is totally contingent on one very big choice we must make.

With that choice in mind, we're going to break down the Mary and Martha story into four main parts. Beginning with *"Lord, Don't You Care?"* we will look at the overwhelming demands we face during the season. Then in *"Worried About*

Much," we'll explore the different distractions we face and how we can approach Christmas differently, while still honoring the traditions we love. We'll also take a closer look in "*Mary Has Chosen*" at the decision she made and consider what changes we'd need to make in order to be both strong enough and committed enough to say yes to Jesus like she did. And finally, in "*The Good Part*," we'll talk about how to keep Christ involved in His own birthday celebration and how we can hold on to the good part or the one thing that can't be taken from us. But first, let's start with something many of us feel during the holiday overload: Martha's cry of "*Lord, Don't You Care?*"

One last thing before we begin, my friends and family would tell you I'm usually not far from a mug of tea. If we were having this conversation in person, I'd be heating the kettle right about now to settle into our discussion. So grab a cuppa (or whatever your cozy cup of comfort might be), and join me as we dig in and uncover the spots where we all tend to stumble, or at least I do, in celebrating Christmas.

CHAPTER ONE

Mary, Martha, and Christmas

The story of Mary and Martha is one you are probably familiar with. But I want to look at it differently here. First, please remember that you are not merely reading a story, or a legend, or mythology, but rather this is actual history, and when Jesus said these words to the sisters, He had each of us already on His heart. The instruction, directly from our Savior, applies just as much today as it did some 2000 years ago. Second, it is no accident that you are reading these scripture verses now.

The Lord sees each one of us and knows our struggles. The distractions in our culture at Christmas rob us of the very joy we want to celebrate, the joy He delivered to the world the night His mother, Mary, delivered Him. Take the time to read it again through a Christmas lens, your Christmas lens. Ask God to show you how you can meet Him in a new and more intimate way this year. Ask Him to show you how to experience this Christmas the way you've always longed for. Therein lies the sure path to the true joy He offers. Joy for the whole world, and right now specifically for you and me.

Now as they were traveling along, He entered a certain village; and a woman named Martha welcomed Him into her home. And she had a sister called Mary, who moreover was listening to the Lord's word, seated at His feet. But Martha was distracted with all her preparations; and she came up to Him, and said, "Lord, do You not care that my sister has left me to do all the serving alone? Then tell her to help me." But the Lord answered and said to her, "Martha, Martha, you are worried and bothered about so many things; but only a few things are necessary, really only one, for Mary has chosen the good part, which shall not be taken away from her." (Luke 10:38–42)

These siblings lived in Bethany, located on the eastern slope of the Mount of Olives. The town stood about one and a half miles east of Jerusalem. Because of its proximity to the Holy City, Bethany was a popular stop on a well-traveled route for pilgrims coming to observe holy days. As such, this village would have been a natural place for Jesus to stop as He and His disciples were probably on their way to the annual Festival of Tabernacles. It is believed that Martha, having heard of Jesus and His upcoming arrival, invited Him to stay at her home. While this was possibly the first encounter of Mary, Martha, and Jesus, scripture goes on to show how close these siblings (and their brother Lazarus) would become with Him.

The Festival of Tabernacles was one of the three major annual observances that Jews celebrated during Jesus' time (along with Passover and Pentecost) as outlined in Deuteronomy 16:16. Each one commemorated an important event in Jewish history. This particular five-day festival, also referred to as The Festival of Booths, continues today and not only celebrates the yearly harvest but also God's continual presence with and provision for the Israelites during their forty years of wilderness wandering.

For the festival, the Jews were required to go to Jerusalem and commemorate their exile history by building temporary "booths." These were simple, open-air shelters, three walls and a roof made from the branches of leafy trees. The pilgrims would then reside in these huts during the festive week, and the city of Jerusalem would have had booths everywhere. According to the law, Jews were required to eat, sleep, pray, and basically dwell in these booths for the entire week (Leviticus 23:40–43). Those who remained at home (mostly the women and children) would also build booths, usually in their home's central courtyard. So, Mary and Martha would have likely built their own booth in their courtyard and would have spent most of their time during that week inside of it and not in the rooms of their actual home. I mention all this because it would have been inside this booth that Jesus was welcomed and that the discourse recorded in the Gospel of Luke would have occurred. Also, the concurrence of the festival and Jesus' visit emphasizes the fact that Martha was hosting Jesus while in the midst of operating in "holiday" festival mode with its added demands for meals, entertaining, and home decor (booths!).

It appears that Martha knew Jesus was coming and probably had started to prepare. But these efforts would have been more exhausting than normal with the necessary running between the house and the booth carrying oil lamps, rugs, cushions, and other supplies. All daily tasks were taken up a notch with running back and forth to grab necessities from the house. And don't forget that Lazarus's helpful hands were probably in Jerusalem for his festival obligations there.

In fact, according to Alfred Edersheim's *The Life and Times of Jesus the Messiah*, it's possible that Jesus was the only guest in Mary and Martha's home that day. He suggests Jesus probably sent His disciples ahead to Jerusalem for the Festival and that Lazarus, as mentioned, had also most likely gone on ahead as well.[1] It is reasonable to assume, though, that a few neighbors or others could have wandered in upon hearing of Jesus' presence.

Initially, Mary was probably helping Martha get ready, but as soon as their guest of honor arrived, the sisters famously chose drastically different responses. As Martha continued to work, I imagine her steps grew heavier and louder, her stares and sighs more glaring and pronounced. All these cues were obviously directed toward Mary, who sat at Jesus' feet, mesmerized with His teaching. As time passed, pots banged and Martha served, she finally reached her breaking point, and the ancient familiar conversation began.

Of course, this conversation didn't go the way Martha had expected and hoped. Jesus, with tenderness and compassion, challenged her for being distracted by things that were not as important as sitting in His presence and learning from Him. He affirmed Mary's choice to sit and listen to His teaching. He went even further and instructed Martha that she should do the same. He told her that being with Him was the right choice, the good choice, and it had value that could never be taken away from her. At no point

---

1   Edersheim, Alfred. *The Life and Times of Jesus the Messiah.* Hendrickson Publishers, 1993.

did He say that what she was doing was not valuable, but rather that it was not the best decision, and its benefit was fleeting.

We can all imagine Martha's frustration and her dilemma. But think about it. She probably wasn't preparing a huge dinner or entertaining a crowd. And honestly, that detail speaks volumes. Because sometimes it doesn't take a dozen guests to feel buried in expectations, it only takes one. It reminds me that at Christmas, it's not just the big events or overflowing schedules that wear us down. It can also be the little quiet things. The pressure we put on ourselves, the mental lists we carry, the weight of wanting everything to be just right. We're not always busy with big things, but we are often worried about much. And that's what Jesus saw in Martha. That's what He still sees in us.

Eventually, they would get hungry and need to eat. How would there be a meal if she didn't prepare one? Why did Mary think she had the right to sit and learn from Jesus instead of helping with the chores at hand? Tired and angry, Martha confidently sought Jesus' help, and His response not only took her by surprise but still challenges us today. In fact, it particularly confronts us at Christmas when the desire to provide a "perfect holiday" for those we love often overrules the desire to sit and joyfully celebrate the birth of our Savior. I have certainly sent glares and banged pots as my hungry loved ones gathered and enjoyed fellowship. Or even worse, I have audibly mumbled frustrations as others have enjoyed their quiet time while I was scrambling their eggs.

When the Lord showed me this similarity, I felt very humbled, very seen, and remarkably loved. Friends, Christmas is and has always been a struggle for me. Martha's frustration and distraction resonate in my heart. When Jesus arrived at her door, she went into warp speed to make the Festival time perfect for Him and any other guests. Sound familiar? Throw in some red and green, and do you see where this is headed? Sure, if it were Christmas week and I went to the door and Jesus was there, well, EVERYTHING would come to a halt. But the reality is that Jesus IS in my home each Christmas and I swirl right past Him, minimizing His presence as I seek to celebrate HIS birthday in MY chosen way. Can I get an AMEN? Further, by the end of the season, I am exhausted, frustrated, and spiritually empty, rather like our frazzled hostess in Luke. There is not another "Hark the Herald" in me, and definitely no joy to wish for the world.

Have you been there?

Ponderings 

- How did you feel at the end of last Christmas?
- What would a Christmas you long for look and feel like?
- What would you like to focus on the most this Christmas?

Lord Don't You Care

I will raise my eyes to the mountains; From where will my help come? My help comes from the Lord, Who made heaven and earth. — Psalm 121:1-2

Help doesn't come from my list, it comes from the Lord.

CHAPTER TWO

Drowning in the Details

When Martha cried out, *Lord, don't You care?* she was desperate (Luke 10:40). It's important to fully grasp the depth of her frustration in that moment, because I think we've all been there. The Greek word *melei*, translated here as *care*, is the exact word the disciples used when Jesus was asleep in the boat while they were being tossed around in a raging storm. The word, specifically, means "care" in the aspect of being aware or even noticing.[2] They were terrified and desperate. They were tossing in the wind, and water was splashing on them and flooding their boat. Any minute, it seemed, they would capsize. Yet Jesus, the Prince of Peace, was sound asleep! Was He not concerned or even aware that they were in imminent danger? They desperately woke Him, and He immediately brought calm.

> And leaving the multitude, they took Him along with them, just as He was, in the boat; and other boats were with Him. And there arose a fierce gale of wind, and the waves were breaking over the boat, so much that the boat was already filling up. And He Himself was in the stern, asleep on the cushion; and they awoke Him and said to Him, "Teacher, **do You not care** that we are perishing?" (Mark 4:36–38)

---

2 Bible Hub. "Strong's Greek 3199 - Melō." *Bible Hub*, https://biblehub.com/str/gn/3199.htm. Accessed 16 Aug. 2025.

Martha likely felt the same way. She had been working so hard to welcome Jesus into her home, making sure everything was just right. All the seasonal prep for the Festival and all the prep to host a meal for her important guest. And yet, it appeared to her that He didn't even seem to notice. Nor did He even pause to acknowledge her effort. **Didn't He care** that she was doing it all alone? Didn't He see how exhausted she was? How could Jesus not even be aware of her sacrifice?

Lord, don't You care? they cried, Martha in the kitchen, the disciples in the storm.

It's funny, and not so funny, how easily we can slip into this holiday martyr mode. We want everything to be magical and meaningful for our families, but somewhere along the way, we go overboard and trade in our peace for pressure. We start to confuse performance with purpose. And honestly, all that clanging and stomping? It's actually a little alarm bell from our soul saying, "I'm doing too much, and I'm running on empty."

Martha wasn't just busy. She was overwhelmed. Distracted. Spiritually depleted. Just like us, when we forget that all the "doing" in the world can't replace the being. Being with Jesus. Being still. Being filled. Like Martha, have you ever banged pots a little harder or stomped through the kitchen a little louder just to make sure everyone knew how hard you were working? I certainly have. In my house, I can be working hard in the kitchen and still see everyone else relaxing in the family room. But my noisy footsteps and frustrated sighs are really little warning signs of what's going on inside me. When I'm spiritually depleted, everything feels heavier. And what spills out of me in those moments reveals just how much I need to return to the One who truly sustains. Because when I'm filled with His peace, I can serve with joy. When our hearts are full of His presence, we don't have to make noise to prove our worth. When we sit at His feet first, the pots can stay quiet, and so can the storm inside us.

Both the disciples at sea and Martha in her kitchen felt exhausted and frustrated. Yet, the emphasis in scripture is their concern that the Lord didn't seem to care. Even though Jesus was right there with them. From our perspective, it might be easy to downplay the disciples' fear. I mean, we know how the story ends. We have a much better understanding of who was in the boat with them. But forget this momentarily and put yourself in their shoes or in Martha's shoes. Both took their focus off Jesus and instead focused on their situation. Their situation became bigger than their faith. Their situation became their focus instead of their faith. Even with Jesus physically in their presence, fear swelled in the boat and anger rose in the kitchen.

Remember, Martha wasn't just frustrated with Mary. She was upset with Jesus, too. He was right there, letting this happen. And isn't it easy to feel that way when things don't go as we think they should or as we think God should allow them? Like the disciples, she also asked for help. But her request was different. Instead of turning to Jesus for safety and peace, she turned to Him with a complaint and an anticipated self-serving outcome. While Jesus calmed the raging storm for the disciples immediately, Martha's storm was in her heart. Martha wasn't drowning as the disciples had feared; her danger was distractions. The Greek word used here, *periespato*, means to be so overburdened by distractions as to be worried and anxious.[3] It is one thing to be busy, but Martha was in such an anxious state of mind that it led her to be so upset that she became critical of Jesus and Mary. She obviously felt left on her own, isolated and unappreciated.

Do you ever feel that way during Christmas? Stuck in the kitchen, buried in wrapping paper, or darting through aisles, wishing you were doing something more life-giving instead? Feeling like everyone else is probably relaxing while you're drowning in your to-do list? I sure have. Every year, two of my friends co-host a Christmas coffee. It's a beautiful, relaxed, drop-in gathering. The kind of event that refuels you, the kind that feels like a little gift tucked into the season. And yet, most years, I tell myself I can't afford the time. I'm too busy checking off my "to-do" list. Has that ever happened to you? That mental state of constant busyness can quietly lead to isolation. It builds up inner frustration. And together, those things slowly drain the joy the season is meant to bring. The kind of joy that being in Jesus' presence provides. The kind of joy that comes from sweet moments of fellowship, like coffee with friends.

Christmas brings a challenge every year. A challenge to resolve the tension between all the busy distractions that come with celebrating and all the deep meaning our hearts are quietly longing to experience. We want to do it all, but we also want to feel something real. As we sort this out together, we'll talk about what it means and how it looks to

---

3   Bible Hub. *Strong's Greek 4049 - Perisseuō. Bible Hub*, https://biblehub.com/str/gn/4049.htm. Accessed 16 Aug. 2025.

spend more time with the Lord, like Mary did. I'm learning that time with Him doesn't necessarily tame the Christmas chaos, but it does teach me to surrender control to the One who brings peace in the middle of it. The One who calls us to rest in His presence, tapping on the sofa for us to sit with Him as we run right by, feeling "unseen"!

But you don't have to feel alone in this. So go ahead and settle in. As my grandchildren say, "Let's get cozy," because we're all in this together. No isolation here, just plenty of grace, tea, and hope for a Christmas that really means something this year.

Now tell me, do you take honey with yours? Sweetener? A splash of milk?

Ponderings 

- Is your Christmas goal or focus based on your personal desire or others' expectations?

- When you feel rushed and or isolated, does it seem like the Lord is far away? Why?

- Think about last Christmas, where did you get off track? Is it the same or different every year?

CHAPTER THREE

No Plug, No Power, No Joy

Ah, the perennial optimism of a new holiday season, especially those years where Thanksgiving falls early, so much time and energy to direct towards all the valued and eagerly awaited annual traditions. Finally, you can listen to all the great Christmas music, and you are convinced and even relieved that it is indeed once again the most wonderful time of the year.

You merrily sing carols and dance around the house as you plan your gift lists, order wrapping supplies, create delicious menus, decide what cookies to bake, and maybe even decorate. And oh, the Christmas card must get done and in the mail, and the house needs to be decorated (which of course means the perfect spruce needs to be selected and lights strung strategically), and you mustn't forget the exterior illumination, which is a big "thing" these days, you know. There are the Christmas movie nights to plan and family gatherings to wedge in between school concerts (which you don't dare leave until everyone has performed). And you certainly don't want to be late starting your Advent calendar. Did you remember the wreaths for the doors?

On top of all this, there are church activities too. (You know, the reason for the season.) There's at least one pageant involving costumes and rehearsals. Often, there are choir concerts involving baking. Additionally, the Advent wreath, with meaningful family devotions preplanned, should be started on time. But hey, you've got this. Energy abounds, to-do lists are inked in red and green, and the perfect Christmas dream is alive as holiday background music cheers you onward. Until sometime, usually towards the end of the second week of all this hap hap happiness, you realize your initial joyful song and dance routine has slowly evolved into more of a desperately determined toy soldier march.

For me, it's like I go to sleep one night feeling settled and on track. Then I wake up the next morning in a parallel universe. This alternate realm, better known as the Land of Missing Essentials, stares me in the face and demands more. More energy, more effort, more perfection. It screams that not only am I way behind, but I've also forgotten all the little extra details. These special touches are mandatory if I want everyone's Christmas experience to be memorable. And I want everyone to feel special, right? So while I continue to monitor the big picture, I also hone in on all the little touches like Christmas sheets on the beds, a welcome home bag of goodies, and you know, all the little things that are suddenly missing essentials. There is also a sudden compulsion to find that PERFECT little something extra for each person to top off their holiday celebration. It's like an out-of-body experience that consumes me and makes me wish I could pull another week out of thin air and add it to the December calendar. With those extra days, I would absolutely be ready for Christmas. This is when, at my house, Advent candles start to go unburned, any daily quiet time I've managed to slip in pretty much disappears, excessive spending ensues as "perfection" decisions are made hastily, and the volume on the now redundant and stress-inducing Christmas tunes is turned down. The worries and distractions are creeping in to overshadow this most joyous of seasons. Yep, I'm drowning in the details once again and joining the Martha express headed directly to Busy Town with no stop for Jesus.

This obsessive compulsion towards an ideal celebration totally reminds me of Clark Griswold in the movie *Christmas Vacation*. He risks life, limb, and ladder to hang 25,000 twinkle lights so his family will feel the wonder of Christmas. No one appears to have requested this or even seems overly interested in the illuminated outcome. Still, he's sweating, stapling, and short-circuiting the entire power grid to provide a magical moment for his family. Yet what happens when his big moment comes? When it is time to present his gift for their holiday cheer. Nothing. Darkness. Frustration. Despair. And why? Because someone flipped the switch off in the garage. All that work, yet completely powerless without the right connection. And isn't that exactly how it feels for us moms? We're untangling lights and expectations, chasing a version of Christmas that feels magical and meaningful. Yet in the midst of all our efforts, we too become unplugged from our source, our Savior. We run ourselves ragged at Christmas. We plan, prepare, purchase, decorate, bake, wrap, schedule, and sprinkle "joy" over everything like it's powdered sugar. But if we've quietly unplugged from our true source, the joy and peace we're chasing won't flow. We may not notice at first while we're too busy buzzing around. But eventually, like Clark standing in the snow with that blank stare, we realize something's missing. It's the connection to our main power source. Just like that switch in the garage had the power to illuminate the whole house, our connection to Jesus is what makes everything else glow. He is the source of the flow of joy that we not only want to share with others, but also want to experience ourselves.

When we stay plugged into Him, joy and peace flow, and we don't exhaust ourselves feeling like we have to produce them. But if we disconnect, even slightly, it shows. We can not create joy for ourselves or others, no matter how hard we try. All the distractions around us pull us into believing that the quality of our family's Christmas depends on what we create. Not only is that not true, but you also don't have to be the electricity that powers everyone's joy this Christmas. Jesus already came to be that. John 15:11 says Jesus spoke His words (referring to keeping His Father's commandments and abiding in His love) so "that My joy may be in you, and that your joy may be made full."

But in the Christmas rush, it's so easy to trade that full joy for a full cart, full calendar, and full-on exhaustion. Real joy, the kind that satisfies, doesn't come from getting everything done, but from staying connected to the One who came to be with us in the first place. When Jesus said this, He had just been teaching the disciples about what it means to abide in Him. So the verse is promising that abiding (spending time with Christ) will lead to a joy that is "full" or complete. This joy is not dependent on external circumstances but arises from an ongoing, consistent relationship with Jesus. When His joy is in us, that is when we are truly joyful. But His joy can only be in us if we are plugged in or abiding with Him.

Are you channeling your inner Clark Griswold every year? Do you feel pulled into a busy rush when you want to experience a more peaceful Christ-centered Christmas personally? I feel like my heart wants to grow closer to the

Lord and spend time in His word, but the world is successfully convincing me of all the things I "need" to do. This annual battle of the commercialism culture competing with our inner desire to personally celebrate a meaningful Christmas is exhausting. It's easy to become frustrated and wonder, like Martha, if Jesus sees what we are going through or if He even cares. Remember, though, He does see and He does care, but we have to be connected to Him ourselves to feel seen and cared for.

This year, before we climb ladders and overfill calendars, let's double-check the switch. Not the one in the garage, the one in our hearts. Is it flipped toward Jesus? Are we connected to the One who dispatches the current of true joy? The One who holds an infinite supply? This season, may our cords fully connect, our cocoa stay hot, and our souls rest in something that definitely lasts. You don't need to climb the roof to make this Christmas bright. Just stay plugged into Him. Also, stay near a warm, cozy mug of tea. Can I top you off?

Ponderings 

- Do you find yourself trying to create a perfect Christmas at the expense of a Christ-centered one?

- Where is your motivation for perfection coming from?

- How can you find joy in a season that seems so rushed?

- Do you feel a need to create joy for your family?

CHAPTER FOUR

Brace Yourself, Christmas is Back

A storm is coming, I'm at the beach, and soon, I will have to evacuate. For generations, my family has been coming to this beach. In fact, it is our escape, a sanctuary of sorts where the massiveness of the ocean has a magical way of putting everything into perspective. It's the perfect place to come alone for some concentrated writing time. Today, the waves, usually calm and rhythmic, have turned wild, crashing into each other in a foamy, white flurry, slamming against the shore like they have something to prove. This coastal storm has been in the forecast for days, expected to bring strong winds and heavy rain. Honestly, though, it's the perfect weather to be inside, curled up and writing (with some hot tea, of course). And that's exactly what I'm doing while the waves explode outside. As I write, I feel confident I am not alone in this ongoing Christmas struggle. Maintaining a focus on Jesus during the upheaval of seasonal demands creates its own choppy mess. The Christmas season, in its own way, is actually another kind of storm. But unlike this beach storm, Christmas doesn't need a forecast. It shows up on our personal radars somewhere between July and November, bringing its gusts of expectations, catalogs, and Instagram temptations. And while I can escape the coastal storm with a well-timed evacuation, there's no avoiding the chaos of the holiday season. If you're anything like me, every year you step into the winds of December with renewed determination. This year, I'm going to celebrate it well! But what exactly does that even mean? More time with family? More time with Jesus? More time with friends? More simplicity, less excess?

I can picture us sitting together, swapping stories about how we've all struggled with the tension between celebrating Christmas culturally and also spiritually. Laughing and encouraging one another with shared stories of frustration. Between the gifts and the gatherings, the traditions and the to-dos, how do we keep Jesus at the center of it all? We cannot treat every aspect of the holiday with equal importance. First, we will run ourselves ragged, totally depleting our joy. Second, when everything is viewed as special or important, we lose sight of and time for the deeply sacred. Friends, Christmas is sacred from top to bottom as it commemorates the holy night of our Savior's birth. It celebrates the night heaven touched earth, and through an infant's birth, hope, grace, and salvation were all born. It's the night God saved the world. And yet, even with all that spiritual significance, somewhere between pulling out the decorations and tying bows on packages, I slip away from Jesus' feet, like Martha, and become totally absorbed in all there is to be done. Sounds crazy, but I bet it also sounds familiar.

Our family was and is very much a Christian family. Our faith is central to who we are, wherever we are. My husband, Bob, and I have always been very involved at church, and the kids were also. We talked about our faith openly at home and stressed the fact that Christmas was first and foremost Jesus' birthday. In 1995, when our children were 3, 7, and 9, this was the inside of our Christmas card:

What is Christmas?

Ashley (9): There are two kinds of Christmas. One that has Santa and trees, cookies, stockings and gifts. And one that's a Christian celebration of Jesus' birthday and a time to be with your family. It's also the Nutcracker!

Bo (7): It's a joyful time when the whole family gets together. People go caroling and we have a big Christmas meal Christmas Eve. It's the time when Jesus was born.

Mac (3): You get toys and make decorations...You praise God...It's the day Santa brings you things...It's the day Jesus was born.

So, while consistently not in first place, Jesus' birthday still made the highlights, even just edging out The Nutcracker. They clearly knew it was Jesus' birthday and also already valued some of our family traditions. However, in their young minds, Santa and Jesus seemed to draw equal attention. As they got older and understood more, they definitely established the meaningful and profound distinction between the two. Yet I would have thought my children knew Jesus was the center of Christmas then, especially the older two. But as I look back, I wasn't making choices totally based on that goal. I wasn't making time for the truly sacred as a priority. I was exhausting myself trying to honor both aspects of Christmas and feeling empty and spent inside. Yes, I know "Santa" can be controversial, and we'll have that conversation later. I loved Santa's annual visits and still do as he comes calling on our grandchildren.

Santa also offers an interesting teaching point to our children, particularly about prayer. Obviously, it's important to point out that Santa isn't God and God isn't Santa. One brings gifts, and the other one is the gift. We shouldn't approach God with a list of things we want, like we do with Santa. Because, unlike Santa, God wants a real relationship with us, not just to fill our stockings. When we're younger, our prayers are often filled with giving thanks, requesting things or help, and blessings for everyone. But as we grow in prayer, our focus shifts. Instead of just pouring our hearts out, we begin to seek God's heart. This is a big shift, and it's necessary for our prayers to mature. We move from wanting things from God, like we might ask Santa for presents, to simply desiring God Himself.

This shift reminds me of Martha's conversation with Jesus. She wanted something from him, but He just wanted her. She wanted him to fix what she saw as a problem. He just wanted her to choose Him before anything else. When Jesus told Martha, "Mary has chosen the good part, which shall not be taken away from her" (Luke 10:42), she must have been shocked. What was the good part that Mary chose? She chose Jesus above anything else. Mary didn't run around "doing for" Jesus; she sat with Him. And He said that was the better choice. He wanted a relationship with her just like He wants one with us today. Even during December, when our hearts are weary and our to-do lists are stacked. Some of this weariness has to be the result of giving every single aspect of Christmas top billing. You just can not attempt this and experience the Christmas your soul longs for. If you chase this goal, and I have, you will have no peace or joy left in your tank by Christmas.

Suddenly, the beach wind is getting louder outside and interrupting my thoughts. The sea foam is swirling, and it's time to pack up and head to Southport, a nearby town, before the powerful winds force the bridge to close. Once there, I'll ride out the storm with friends. That's what I want to do with you, also. Ride out this whirlwind storm of Christmas together. Even as I prepare to leave, I'm eager to continue this conversation with you about what the Lord is teaching me. Not just about surviving the chaos of Christmas, but about thriving in spite of it. About growing spiritually and being filled, even as we pour into the many people around us. Navigating the season while reflecting outwardly, and at the same time feeling inwardly, the joy of God's gift to the world. Can this be accomplished? I feel the Lord softly telling us both that it can. What is the Lord whispering? Well, the answer might not be what you'd think, but then again, what else could it be? But we are getting ahead of ourselves. More tea?

Ponderings 

- When do you start to prepare for Christmas? How do you start?

- Have you ever thought about preparing spiritually for Christmas? What would it look like?

- What would a list of priorities look like for you this season?

CHAPTER FIVE

A Mary Heart in a Martha Season

I've always felt a bond with other moms heading into the Christmas season. Sort of a "ready, set, go" mentality as each December approaches. It's as if we're comrades starting a marathon, but sprinting from the very first step. Our expectations, or at least mine, often far exceed our actual capabilities. We strive to create the perfect joyful holiday for our families, only to end up exhausted, spiritually drained, and falling into the same post-Christmas New Year's resolutions. We're going to slow down, be more disciplined with our quiet time, and finally stick to our self-improvement goals. But let's not analyze THAT today. Instead, let's back up and rethink the whole unfortunate mindset of just "surviving" Christmas.

For years, one of my favorite Christmas traditions was delivering fun gifts to friends to help mark the beginning of "the season." This "broad" list consisted of women I saw very little of, but missed, and women I thankfully saw more often. The gifts were always practical and corny. For example, one year they received a set of napkin rings with a tag that read, "It's time to ring in the season." Another year, it was spatulas saying, "It's time to stir things up." Another year, it was a koozie with a caffeinated can drink and a tag saying, "Wake

UP, it's starting!" You get the idea. It gave me and others, I hope, a sense of community that we were all in this season together and poked fun at the craziness ahead. I got the biggest kick out of this, but stopped after six or so years to concentrate more on family traditions.

If we indeed do the math, though, there's nothing about Christmas that should bring on the stress of a marathon. Did I actually just say that? Stop and think about Mary and Joseph that first Christmas night. They searched desperately for a place to stay after a long, hard, dusty journey. Mary endured childbirth amongst the animals, and shortly after, they even unexpectedly hosted shepherds. THAT was a marathon and stressful for sure. Yet in God's perfect plan, every challenge they faced brought about the greatest gift the world has ever received. Their obedience had certainly been stressful, but its result allows us to celebrate from a place of total joy today. Obedience is an important part of our relationship with Christ. Being obedient to God means aligning our actions, thoughts, and heart with His will, even when it's uncomfortable, inconvenient, or unclear, as it was for Mary and Joseph. It's not about just following directions; it's more about walking in loving trust, like when Jesus said, "If you love Me, you will keep My commandments" (John 14:15). Obedience isn't about control; it's about a connection based on love. Because all the true work of Christmas was done long ago, today, we are left to receive and celebrate the eternal gift that each of us has been given.

You might be thinking, well, of course, the first Christmas was that way, but I'm not exactly planning to host a nativity in my home. I'm aiming to provide the setting for a joyful celebration of our Savior's birth. Well, me too! Careful, though, this is where there can be a real shift from a Mary Christmas to a Martha Christmas. We will be referring to this as "the tilt." It's hardly a pivot because the perspective change can be so tiny. Just like Martha, we can spend so much time on all the preparations that we don't have time left to spend with Jesus. While this is always a poor choice, it is especially so at Christmas. It keeps us from receiving the very thing only He can give us, joy. And joy is exactly what we need in order to experience the Christmas we've been longing for. You see, we must not lose sight of where the seeds of boundless joy come from. Sustained joy doesn't come from the fun of decorating and shopping and baking, even when it is for others and even when we enjoy it. These activities can make us happy as we are preparing a wonderful time for our loved ones. But that happiness fades as we become stressed with all there is to do. We become exhausted and spiritually dry personally by trying to produce joy for everyone's holiday. Because the cost of doing "all the things" is usually not having time left to sit with Jesus. In other words, there is no time for Him to renew us spiritually. Remember, you can't keep giving what you don't have. Joy is not something we can produce and give. For Mary and Joseph, joy didn't come from their struggles. It came from their obedience to God and their relationship with God. Ours comes the exact same way. We can rest in the truth that Christmas isn't about what we do, but about what He has done. When we shift our focus from our performance to His presence (a Mary tilt), we find the peace and joy that Christmas was always meant to bring.

The Christmas season isn't meant to be orchestrated by us at all, but rather to be received from Him. Our overzealous, imaginative plans come from a good place, though, a desire to reflect the image of our infinitely creative God. But somewhere along the way, our methods have hijacked our focus. Instead of centering on the gift Himself, Jesus, our efforts often become a grand showcase of our own abilities. There is a subtle shift when it becomes less about Jesus and more about how my house looks, my food tastes, and how many gifts are under my tree. We shift from sitting in His presence, celebrating His birth, to perfecting the celebration itself, often, if we're honest, to impress others. In other words, a Martha tilt.

We pour ourselves into the details, curating the perfect Christmas experience, decked-out decorations, fancy tables topped with delicious meals, and an abundance of gifts under the tree. And while none of these things are bad, they can quietly shift our hearts from worship to performance, from receiving to striving, and from spiritual joy to spiritual fatigue. And Heaven forbid we don't get the appreciation we think our efforts warrant, also!

But here's the beautiful irony: the very first Christmas was anything but curated. It was raw, unpolished, and completely out of human control. Mary and Joseph didn't orchestrate the setting, the visitors, or the timeline. They showed up, weary and obedient, faithfully receiving the miracle. Do you think they wondered if the Lord genuinely cared when there wasn't a place for them to stay? When things weren't easy, but were very difficult along the way? Scripture suggests that they trusted God and tells us of their faithful walk with God. Their faith and God's faithfulness both show us that God indeed does care. Their obedience provides our invitation to lay down the exhausting effort of making Christmas perfect. We can instead step into the wonder of what's already been done for us. Shifting our behavior from doing to being and from fatigue back to joy. Not just surviving all the to-dos but thriving in all that's been done. Not wondering if the Lord sees us, but making sure we see Him.

So what makes this so hard? Perhaps, like Martha, we are worried about too much. Perhaps we are putting the urgent in front of the important. How we spend our time should draw us closer to the Lord and not distract us from Him. So, what do we do?

Let's stretch and refill our mugs so we can discuss the distractions that keep us from Jesus. So far, we've wondered if His eyes were on us. "Lord, don't You care?" Perhaps we've got it backward. Are our eyes on Him?

Ponderings 

- What exhausts you the most about Christmas?

- Do you feel stuck in a pattern of endless "to-dos" at Christmas?

- What could you change so that you felt you received Christmas this year instead of producing it?

Worried About Much

Having cast all your anxiety on Him, because He cares about you.
— 1 Peter 5:7

Your worries aren't yours to carry. His shoulders are strong enough.

CHAPTER SIX

I'm Tired, But the Table is Beautiful

It's the most wonderful time of the year, until it isn't. Right? The thought of festive parties, marshmallow toasting, and caroling in the snow sounds magical, but in reality, the holiday cheer often gets buried under endless to-do lists, gift wrapping, and meal prep. The fun festivities become "to-dos" themselves. Getting the house fully decorated takes time and effort, and by the time I've placed the last piece of greenery, I'm already behind on baking or shopping and scrambling to catch up. In fact, as the stress levels rise, I gradually swap out the festive, fast-tempo tunes for instrumental Christmas music, anything without a single "fa la la" or overly jingly beat. It feels like I'm running nonstop right up until we leave for church on Christmas Eve. Then, as soon as we're back home, it's straight into last-minute prep mode, wrapping those final gifts and making sure everything is just right. At some point, exhaustion sets in, but there's no time to slow down. The anticipation keeps everything in motion, carrying me forward until the moment finally arrives. Christmas morning. The magic, the wonder, the excitement, for a little while. And then, inevitably, someone says it, "I'm hungry!"

I can be calm and content in the moment, but that peace is shaken quickly during Christmas. Let's face it, there is always something to be done, or someone hungry, or someplace to be during this season. As our inner joy is depleted, happy moments do appear occasionally, but unlike inner joy, those moments can be gone in a second, like when someone says again, "I'm hungry!"

I love a celebration, and time around the table is always special. Whether celebrating a birthday, a holiday, or friendship, gathering to share a meal is a way to be present for each other. Many of my favorite times with friends and family happen around a festively decorated table, sharing a delicious meal. Further, at Christmas, there's something significant and special about gathering multiple generations of our family for a meal, where stories are told, laughter is shared, and memories are made. It's as if time stands still when we're gathered around the table, and for those moments, the only thing that truly matters is the people sitting there with you. And every year, as I finally settle into my seat, the long-awaited, much-anticipated moment arrives, the deeply felt and deeply satisfied sigh. The rush is over, the table is full, and for the first time all season, I can just be.

After all the running around, the late-night wrapping, and the endless grocery store trips, there's finally a pause. A deep breath. A chance to just take it all in and be fully present. The laughter, the warmth, the sticky fingers and giggles, it all wraps around me, and for the first time, I let myself soak it up. And that's when it hits me, how blessed I am, how much this all means, and what a true gift Christmas is.

But wait. Just yesterday I was wishing another driver a not-so-cheery "Ho Ho Ho" with my Ho Ho Horn, and before that I was dropping off gifts at dear friends' homes quietly hoping they weren't there because I honestly did not have the time to visit. Not exactly the spirit of Christmas! My level of stress was dramatically outperforming my level of joy. It always seems like all the last-minute details do their best to crowd out any remaining jingle in my bells. So what suddenly changed at the table Christmas afternoon? What finally brought the peace that had pretty much evaded me all season? Did life pause, or did I finally press pause?

There I was, sitting with the ones I love, fully present in the moment. No distractions, no double-tasking, just us, together. And in that stillness, I felt it: peace, comfort, and a deep sense of belonging. This was what I had been longing for, what I had been racing toward all along. And yet, even this, this beautiful moment, pales in comparison to the peace I could have chosen to focus on all season long. What if I had said yes to Him, to stillness, to His presence, from the very beginning?

You see, sitting at the table, I felt worldly peace or happiness. It's wonderful, but it's also fleeting. It shifts as quickly as our circumstances do. The calm around the Christmas table could vanish in an instant with a spilled drink, a dropped plate, or an unexpected disagreement. And soon enough, the messy kitchen and looming cleanup would remind me of my exhaustion, nudging that satisfying but temporary peace aside. It doesn't take much for worldly peace to slip through our fingers. That's what we need to remember and to remind each other: this kind of peace isn't the peace Jesus offers. It doesn't even come close. The satisfaction of a job well done or the joy of a beautifully set table is good, but temporary. The peace that comes from being in the presence of the Lord? That's unshakable. It can't be undone by a mess, an unexpected setback, or a change in circumstances. It's the kind of peace that stays, no matter what. It's peace from the Prince of Peace.

In our scripture on Mary and Martha, we clearly see that our Lord truly does care. He cares deeply as He addresses Martha so tenderly. While He indeed gives us the power to choose, He very much desires that we choose Him. He values time with us and wants us to always choose to spend time with him. If we start there, the rest of the day's cares will fall into place. But how do we prepare ourselves to make the better choice daily, to desire the right thing? Especially through the Christmas season?

First, we must recognize that deeper faith and its resulting joy won't come to us just because we desire it. While that seems obvious, it is easy to live as though it would work. Instead, both are the result of a commitment to the discipline of pursuing them. We pursue them by pursuing Jesus. We pursue Jesus by spending time with Him. Finally, we can only spend time with Him if we choose to prioritize our relationship with Him over everything else. Seeking God first brings order to our lives. I think most of us can agree that the days we begin by spending time with Jesus have an order about them, and we, in turn, have an inner strength about us. Scripture even teaches us that by waiting on the Lord (spending time with the Lord), our strength is renewed, we can even mount up like eagles to run and not be weary and walk and not be faint (Isaiah 40:31).

Again, this is where Mary and Martha chose differently. And yes, I know I keep repeating myself, but that's because

I'm trying to emphasize that the first step to a more joyful Christmas is basically a choice. It's not a simple one, though. As we get into this new section, we must start here by realizing the difference between happiness and true joy. Most of the world settles for happiness, but you're reading this book because you know there's more. There's better. There's Jesus. Further, the difference between the two choices is magnified during the holidays. We will move on shortly to discover how committed we have to be to stick to what can be a constantly challenged choice.

If we were sitting together right now, I'd be reheating the tea kettle as we've started digging deeper into this struggle. Because let's be honest, hot tea just makes everything feel a little cozier. And trust me, things are about to heat up even more as we get to the root of what we've been getting wrong about Christmas. And I do mean we. Even with plenty of Christmases under my belt, I still fall short. Every year, I find myself relearning the same lesson. The struggle is real, but so is our Savior, very real. Tea anyone?

Ponderings 

- What would Mary and Martha's choices look like today for Christmas?

- What would Jesus say that you are too worried about at Christmas?

- When are your true moments of joy during the Christmas season?

CHAPTER SEVEN

Happy Birthday to Who?

If you're reading this book, I'm guessing you love celebrations and birthdays as much as I do. Especially, as we've just discussed, when celebrating involves gathering with friends and family around the table. Some of my best memories are wrapped up in these moments of good food, good conversation, and the kind of laughter that makes your side hurt. And then, there's Christmas! From the classic red and green colors to the choruses of well-known carols filling the air, don't you want to experience every part of it? You would think these two loves, celebrating people and celebrating Christmas, would naturally go hand in hand. But for a lot of us, the combination is combustible. The season gives us permission to go overboard on our favorite things, and as we all know, too much of a good thing, well, is not always a good thing. I can almost picture Jesus standing there with a knowing smile, lovingly shaking His head: "*Martha Martha...*"

When I celebrate a family member's or friend's birthday, it takes time and effort, but the focus always stays on them. The party is for them. The table decorations, the cake, the gifts, everything centers around the person we're celebrating. At the end of the day, I feel confident that they feel loved, honored, and appreciated. For example, all of my grandchildren, so far, have summer birthdays. Ashley, my daughter who is affectionately called Ash Ash by her nieces and nephews, throws a big birthday bash at the beach each summer for all of them together. This is an all-out themed meal and cake with decorations, etc. Even though we're celebrating all four kids at once (plus their two dads), everyone feels completely loved and seen. It's pure joy, and we all look forward to it every year. Ashley's amazing at making them all feel special. She keeps her focus on who she is celebrating.

But how do we make Jesus feel special for His birthday? Admittedly, it doesn't help that He isn't physically here to blow out birthday candles or unwrap gifts. We can't see His face light up or hear Him say, "Wow, thank you!" Celebrating Him takes faith and effort. It's not as easy or straightforward as planning a beach birthday party where I can see my grandkids' smiles and hear their squeals of delight. When my granddaughters, Sarah and Macy, celebrate their birthdays, there is usually a tutu involved and definite vibes of "I'm the birthday girl." Jesus doesn't actually run around giving off that vibe! Somehow, we get caught up in the more, more, and more that is screaming all around us while Jesus gently whispers for us to be still. I think that's part of why I end up so distracted. It's not that I don't want to honor Jesus; I sincerely do. But all my good intentions somehow shift into a blur of shopping, planning, and trying to make everything just right for the people I can visibly see. And before I know it, I've spent more time stressing over the season than personally rejoicing over the Savior, Jesus Christ, who became man, and the magnitude of what that means.

I hope that because of our conversation so far, you're catching this shift, the Mary to Martha tilt. When our focus leaves Jesus, it goes to everything else that's calling with urgency or providing visual satisfaction. The only way to stay focused is to start focused (like Mary) and never leave His presence. Because, oh boy, the shift happens so fast. Before I finish one thing, I'm distracted by the next. Right? The to-do list grows, and the Post-it notes are scattered everywhere. Somehow, without even realizing it, I get scattered everywhere, too. I'm scattered mentally and physically by the shopping, planning, and my endless checklists. Then I find myself mumbling like Martha, *Lord, don't You care?* Do you see how much I'm doing? Why do You feel so far away? Can't you just see Jesus shaking His head, looking back at me, saying, "Ann, Ann, *you are worried about many things...and you are not choosing the best thing.*"

It all sounds so obvious and easy when you read the scripture, but at Christmas especially, it is so hard not to be wrapped up in distractions. Our culture makes it so attractive to decorate, bake, dress, and celebrate well in every way. My focus on Jesus gets lost in the rush of chasing the perfection standard. But again, why, when it comes to celebrating Jesus' birthday, is it so different from all the other birthdays we honor? Why do we get so distracted over and over again, year after year? Yes, it's certainly harder since we can't see Him to celebrate Him. But maybe another part of the problem is that celebrating Jesus feels so big. I mean, we're talking about honoring the Savior of the world. That's intimidating. It feels like we should be doing something huge, something impressive, to show how much we love Him. Our usual default, then, is to express His love by loving others. Gift giving at Christmas is a wonderful way to reflect God's love for us with our love for each other. But before you know it, we have also added excessive gifts, grand meals, beautiful settings, festive clothes, and holiday entertaining. All those good intentions turn into stress and pressure. Part of this shift is certainly due to our Instagram-driven culture and our obsession with perfection.

When my husband, my children, or my mom has a birthday, I just ask them what they want. Boom. Easy. But Jesus? What do you get for the King of Kings? He doesn't have a wish list, at least not one that I can check off on Amazon. And besides, thinking about Jesus' birthday list, that's a tough, deep, soulful question to sit with. So, instead of wrestling with it, my brain takes the easy way out. Diving straight into shopping, decorating, planning, and suddenly, I'm happily off to the races.

But shouldn't we stop and ponder what Jesus would want for His birthday? We've talked about our typical birthday celebrations and how they remain focused on the person being honored. But for Jesus? If Christmas were really about Him, I'd be starting each morning in December with Him, seeking His heart. Devotedly spending as much time as possible with Him. Instead, I'm usually scrambling for last-minute stocking stuffers, wondering if we have food that everybody likes, and attending various holiday events, none of which pay tribute to Jesus in any way. At the time when I most want to honor Him, I am also the most distracted from Him. Meanwhile, He's standing at the door of His own party, waiting for me to acknowledge Him while I busily stress over whether my family will like their gifts. Sounds like Martha running around busily serving Jesus instead of giving Him what He genuinely desired, her presence. Honestly, I know I have to be more intentional. Jesus isn't going to just pop out of the nativity scene and force me to celebrate Him. I have to decide that His birthday matters more than the chaos, even the fun chaos. I also have to live out that decision.

Truthfully, if we treated anyone else's birthday like we treat Jesus' birthday, it would be ridiculous. Imagine throwing a party but getting so caught up in the decorations, food, and party favors that you barely acknowledge the actual birthday person. Or maybe you do, kind of. Maybe you mumble a quick "Happy Birthday" before rushing off to check on the appetizers. That's exactly what we tend to do to Jesus. Sure, we read about the first Christmas from Luke's Gospel every Christmas Eve. This is after we've attended a Christmas Eve service and even enjoyed a birthday cake for Jesus. But if we're honest, it often feels a little obligatory.

Somewhere along the way, I've turned His birthday into my own production, packed with my own expectations that leave me exhausted instead of joyful. This is just crazy, though, because the truth is, celebrating Jesus should be the easiest birthday of all. He doesn't desire presents, a perfect meal, or an Instagram-worthy setting. He just wants us. Maybe this year, I'll finally be successful in giving Him exactly that.

Going all in on celebration and generosity isn't necessarily bad. It just needs the right foundation. In fact, the desire to celebrate Christmas extravagantly comes from a beautiful place. We're honoring God's greatest gift to the world. The problem isn't that we celebrate, it's how we celebrate. We love making birthdays special for the people we care about, and that's a good thing! But somehow, when it comes to Jesus, the One whose birthday totally changed all eternity, we miss the mark and let the chaos take over. This is such an unfortunate swap and a definite Martha tilt.

The to-do lists, the expectations, the constant running around, they all pull our focus and begin to drain our joy before we even realize it. These things are distractions. Distractions are what we worry about and fuss over that can be fun, but also can take our focus off of Jesus. And where did I get the idea that putting Jesus first would take all the fun out of Christmas? It absolutely makes it better. When we slow down and celebrate Him the way we really want to, there's more joy, more peace, and way less stress.

But the best part is that this joy overflows. We love people better, give more freely, and we spread the kind of Christmas cheer that lasts beyond December. What a gift that is, not just for us, but for our families too. When they see us fully celebrating Jesus, without the stress, the pressure, or the need for perfection, it gives them permission to do the same. Maybe this is the year we finally do this. We celebrate His birthday intentionally, celebrating Him, and finally enjoy it more than ever.

This will mean giving Him time before anything else. That's before the daily to-dos, before the stress, before the madness takes over. It will also mean remaining in His presence throughout everything we do that day. Bringing Him with us so we are able to stay focused on what is important. Stop and think about what a blessing that is. And here's another challenge. Do we know Jesus the way we know our closest family and friends? Do we have the kind of intimacy with Him that lets us confidently say, I know exactly what He would want for His birthday? Because if we don't, then maybe our Christmas distractions are in fact revealing something bigger. Maybe, without realizing it, we've let other things, or people, take first place in our hearts. Maybe we've placed our love for the holiday above our love for Him. I love Jesus so dearly, but perhaps my actions are showing me I love some other things or people more. Maybe it's time to admit we all have some idols that we are placing before the Lord. Ouch.

Let's not beat ourselves up, though. Flip it around and look at it this way. Each distraction gives us an opportunity to turn back to God! I think about the Grinch and how he finally understood Christmas. You know, the story of the Grinch and the story of Mary and Martha actually have a lot in common. Both show what happens when we get caught up in all the stuff, the distractions, whether it's stealing it like the Grinch or trying to perfect it like Martha. The Grinch gets annoyed by all the noise, the chaos, and the ridiculous joy. He thinks if he can just remove the decorations, the gifts, and the roasted beast, he can silence the happy. Martha, in her own way, is doing the same thing. Instead of getting rid of bothersome noise, though, she's trying to create the perfect environment for Jesus, but in doing so, she ends up missing time with Jesus herself. Both the Grinch and Martha miss the whole point of what's right in front of them. Just like we can provide the perfect setting for our family, but in the process, we never have time to personally spend with them. What I love about both stories is the gentle wake-up call they offer. The Grinch thought Christmas was all about the stuff, and Martha thought worship was all about the service, but both missed the heart of it. Mary, however, like the Whos in Whoville, got it. Even today, she would know that Christmas is totally about presence, not perfection. Being at Jesus' feet was her choice over everything. And when the Grinch heard singing on Christmas morning, it undid him. He finally got it, though, and his heart grew. And every year, I have to remind myself of that, too. My heart doesn't need more tasks and to-dos, or in other words, distractions.

You and I are indeed worried about much. And all that worry pulls our attention in a million directions. Before we realize it, we've drifted into a full Martha tilt. And honestly, the most frustrating part is we know we're doing it. We feel it. But we do it anyway. We need to spend some time on this.

So let's pause here for a second.

Think about it. When I keep saying yes to things I already know are going to steal my time, drain my energy, and rob me of peace, it's not just me being a little "busy." It's me slowly letting myself get consumed, and in the process, quietly scooting Jesus out of the picture. I'll tell myself, "I'll spend time with Him later," but we all know how that usually goes. Later turns into never, especially around Christmas when every moment feels like it's already spoken for. The tricky part is that a lot of these distractions seem harmless. Things like planning the perfect family gathering or scrolling for the best stocking stuffers. But when I start chasing those things more than I'm chasing time with Jesus, I've moved Him out of first place in my life. That's not just a distraction anymore, that's a replacement. That's an idol.

It's sobering to say it out loud, but it's true: when I knowingly choose things that push Jesus to the side, I'm not just overwhelmed, I'm worshiping something else. And that's definitely not the Christmas we want to experience. It is definitely not producing the Christmas we long for, either. We are going to lean into this a little more because now we're getting into the heart of it. We've got some honest, meaningful things to talk through, and it might not be easy. Let's not rush. Go ahead and pour yourself another cup of tea. Pause, sip, reflect, and when you're ready, we'll move on together.

Ponderings 

- What do you think would be on Jesus' Christmas/Birthday list?

- If you were indeed planning a birthday party for Jesus, what would it be like?

- What gets in the way (distracts) and keeps you from knowing Jesus better?

CHAPTER EIGHT

Stuck on Christmas Repeat

So, we've just started to unpack what I think is the biggest reason so many of us end up completely worn out and disappointed spiritually by Christmas. And while I was praying this through and piecing it together, I had to laugh. I realized I've been doing the very thing they did. The thing that I always shake my head at when I read their story in the Bible. Whose story, you ask? What thing?

It's the Israelites. If you've ever spent much time in the Old Testament, you might be familiar with the cyclical behavior of this nation of God's chosen people. Their behavior has always puzzled me and also brought criticism from me. For generations, the nation would pledge its allegiance to God and not only claim but brag about its covenant relationship with Him. But as soon as they felt any reason to doubt God, they immediately made idols to worship. As soon as they didn't hear from God or feel His favor, they would reach for something tangible to praise. How could anyone be so shortsighted? How could they literally witness miracles, seas parting, manna falling from the sky, water gushing from rocks, and then still turn around and worship something they made with their own hands? A golden calf? Really? Then, with the passing of time, they would realize the seriousness of their mistake and pledge allegiance to God again. Only to repeat the same pattern once more. Every single time.

For years, I've read their story with this mix of fascination and frustration. How could they forget so quickly? How could their loyalty and trust in God shift so fast, time after time? They'd experience His faithfulness one moment and then go chasing after something shiny the next. But recently, the Lord nudged my heart. He tenderly called me out ("Martha, Martha") and showed me that this is exactly what I do every Christmas. Another Ouch!

The truth is, I wrestle with idols all year long. I just didn't realize it. But around Christmas? It's like they come out in full force, wearing glitter and wrapped in pretty paper. And the thing is, they're usually good things! Family time, gift giving, and fun traditions. All good stuff. But when they start taking up more of my heart than Jesus? When my peace depends more on how the living room looks than on who my Savior is. That's when I know I've drifted. Again. The Martha tilt.

I know I can't be the only one. We've already acknowledged how challenging Christmas can be. The expectations. The distractions. The noise. The temptation to chase after everything but the One whom the season is actually about. And every year, I find myself in the same situation and the same inward battle.

I think we all do. We declare that God is everything to us and that He alone is enough. But then life happens. Stress creeps in. Doubt whispers. Before we know it, we are reaching for something, anything, to hold on to. Now I've never melted down jewelry or silver to create a statue, but I do establish idols in other ways, and I bet you do too.

Not the golden-calf kind, but the everyday things that we quietly allow to take up more space in our hearts than God.

Because if we're honest, we don't always recognize them for what they are. So how do we know if something has become an idol? Here's a simple question to ask: What am I running toward first? When I'm stressed, do I go to God, or do I scroll my phone, grab another cup of coffee (I could NOT bring myself to say tea), or try to control everything around me? When I'm feeling insecure, do I seek God's truth or do I look for validation from others? When life feels overwhelming, do I pray, or do I fill my schedule with distractions?

An idol is anything that takes up more of my thoughts, time, or trust than Jesus. It's the thing I think I need to be okay. And as mentioned already, it's usually a good thing, like family or even ministry. But when a good thing takes God's place, it becomes the wrong thing. When a good thing becomes an ultimate thing, we have a problem. And we all know there are lots of good things at Christmas that we can unknowingly and very easily place before Jesus. Usually, the stress of the season invites all our tempting idols to the surface, offering fake momentary relief. This can be in the form of a new holiday dress, an extra present for a loved one, some new placemats, or even indulging in holiday treats. The list continues with whatever your go-to in December is that promises a quick hit of satisfaction or control in a season that can feel like it's slipping through our fingers. But here's the catch: none of these options successfully fills us. They distract us. They soothe us for a moment, then leave us even more depleted. And if we're not careful, we start leaning on them instead of the One who came to bring real peace.

It's not that these things are bad on their own. The problem is when we start turning to them first. When they become our comfort, our reward, or our escape, that's when a sweet moment of celebration can quietly shift into worshiping the wrong thing. And the season that's supposed to draw us nearer to Christ ends up pulling us farther away. And once again, we have missed the Christmas we long for.

Year after year, we all start with such good intentions. This Christmas, we say, I'm going to keep my heart centered and I'm going to focus on Jesus. And we mean it! But then, the season starts picking up speed. Suddenly, we're searching online, trying to track down the last size of those pajamas that have to match (for Christmas photos, obviously), and hunting to remove that one strand of lights that all of a sudden isn't twinkling. And somewhere along the way, without even realizing it, we start chasing perfection, more than His presence. We chase visible coziness over Christ. Magical over meaningful. And let's be real, we start thinking if everything doesn't look just right, we've somehow failed Christmas and our loved ones. It's like we mentioned earlier, we focus on what we can see, and it consumes us quickly. Especially now with Instagram and social media constantly telling us that perfection is not only possible but even showing us what it looks like. But here's the thing. If we can stay alert, we can catch it. If we can focus, we won't become frantic. We can pull back before we're in full idol mode.

And one simple question can help us put the brakes on, focus, and stop us in our tracks: "What am I chasing?" Because whatever we're chasing is what we're worshiping. Is it peace? Control? Approval? Perfection? A feeling? A flawless family memory? Or is it the Savior who came quietly, humbly, and without a single string of lights? We can reset. We can resist the pull. And we don't have to do it perfectly. We just have to keep turning our hearts back toward the One who never stops chasing us.

Am I more focused on creating the perfect holiday than on worshiping the perfect Savior? Do I feel like Christmas is ruined if things don't go the way I planned? Am I finding my joy in traditions, gifts, and preparations instead of in Christ? Do I feel anxious, stressed, or frustrated because I'm trying to control all the details? Here's the hard truth: Anything we feel we "must have" for Christmas to feel right, other than Jesus, is probably an idol. Ouch.

Let's let that sink in. For me, it hits home. For me, it's a wake-up call. Does it speak to you and to your experience?

No one wants to think they're making an idol out of their holiday traditions, but let's be real. How often do we stress more about giving the magical Christmas experience than we do about drawing nearer to Christ? We'll sacrifice sleep, money, and sanity to make everything perfect, but how much effort are we putting into just being with Jesus? I'm definitely chasing the perfect Christmas more than the Prince of Peace. Double Ouch.

Might be a good time for some fresh air. I feel like I'm beating myself up, and that's not my intention for you or me.

We must not forget the good news! Jesus came to free us from all of this. He didn't come, so we could create the perfect holiday for Him. Just the opposite! He came because we can't make ourselves or anything perfect. Christmas isn't about us getting it all right. It's about a Savior who has made us right with God. None of the aspects of Christmas that we love are bad; they can all be wonderful parts of celebrating the season. It's just when they push Jesus to the side in our hearts, they become something else entirely. They become idols.

And just like the Israelites, we find ourselves back in the same place. Yet, we realize year after year that nothing fully satisfies but Him. So maybe instead of shaking our heads at these people from centuries ago, we should let their story be a mirror. A reminder that our hearts are prone to wander. And that, even despite our fickle ways, God never gives up on His people. That's the part that gets me every time. No matter how many times they turned away, no matter how deep their rebellion went, God still took them back. Still pursued them. Still loved them.

And He does the same for us.

Every single time.

So let's take a breath. This is a good moment to stretch or take a walk. There is a lot to reflect on here. Together, I hope we can agree on how easily idols can sneak into our hearts, especially when we're not even looking for them. They're subtle, but they're there. Let's gently, but honestly, name them and let Jesus meet us right in the middle of it all. Help yourself to more tea! This ole gal needs a bathroom break!

Ponderings 

- What do you chase at Christmas?

- What good things become idols for you at Christmas?

- How can you be prepared this year to fight the traditional idols that you chase at Christmas?

CHAPTER NINE

Balancing the Feast and the Faith

Let's talk a little more about idols. Even just the word idol sounds evil and extreme. When I hear the word, I picture golden calves or strange metallic statues with people bowing down and offering sacrifices. Is that what comes to your mind too? Honestly, that's exactly what the enemy wants us to picture, something extreme and distant from our reality. He doesn't want us to have any clue that we are capable of idol worship. Satan is sneaky and crafty in ways we don't expect. He doesn't show up with horns and a pitchfork; he works through distractions, busyness, and anything that shifts our focus off the Lord. Idolatry just looks different these days.

And what better time for the enemy to work than Christmas? Can't you picture his delight in watching us run ourselves ragged? He's thrilled with our weariness and our frustration. Why? Because it keeps us from the One who is our joy. The One who gives rest to our souls. For so long, I didn't see it. I was blind to how often and how easily I got pulled into all the distractions of the season. Further, I didn't honestly know it was such a bad thing. It all seemed fun until it all became too much. What I did know was that Christmas was not working for me, and I desperately wanted to fix it.

Let's recap for a second. We have discussed that Christmas is a struggle for many of us and learned from our scripture that Jesus definitely cares, and it's not what He wants for us. He gently reminds us that, like Martha, we are indeed worried and distracted with many things. So now, as we figure out how to sort out these distractions and stay focused in the midst of them, we need to look honestly within ourselves.

What are the distractions that pull you during the season? Are they things that you enjoy doing usually or just at Christmas? Are there some things you do just because you always have? Do your efforts bring you joy, or feel obligated? Are there some things you do for the sake of your family that you personally don't enjoy working on? Digging deeper, are your efforts coming from a place of pride? Or are they the result of insecurity and a desire to prove something? Trying to impress others with what you are capable of? Does your home say "Look what I can do"? Or does it say "Welcome, I'm glad you're here"? This, by the way, is a question from your perspective, not your guests. What does it say to you? Do you spend more time decorating than you do enjoying? Are you even capable of enjoying your holiday home, or do you constantly see something else that needs to be done? And all these questions just pertain to our home!

Do your presents need to be beautiful with big festive bows? Do your tables have to be flawless? What about your meals? Your clothes? Your gifts? Do you need to be seen at all the parties? What other distractions pull at you that become overwhelming instead of enjoyable?

Finally, pause here and think about this. Do you feel you have started to serve the season and not the Savior? If so, that's also when the distractions, either individually or combined, have become idols. Each one of these tasks is fun for me, and that's why Christmas is a combustible combination I have to navigate. They are all natural components of our celebrations, but the problem is that our culture calls us to be perfect at each one of them. And that's the noise we hear over Jesus' still calm voice that calls us back to Him.

I'm sure you have learned for yourself that there is a cost to listening to the world's noise.

The first thing I've lost? Time with the Lord. We've already mentioned those morning moments as the season wears on, when you crawl out of bed, already feeling behind, and tell yourself, "I'll get to my quiet time later." Yeah, right.

The second thing I've lost is time with my family. Isn't that ironic? Just like Martha with Jesus, I'm doing so much for them that I don't have time to just be with them. Admittedly, sometimes that's just life. But often, it's a sign my priorities have slipped out of alignment and I've made a Martha tilt following the lure of holiday perfection.

Christmas is a time of year when we want to be happy, and we want those around us to be happy too. And honestly, we should be overflowing with joy! After all, we're celebrating the moment God sent His Son to rescue us and offer us eternal life. That's not just good news, it's the best news. And we want to celebrate it in our hearts. Yet, the only obstacle getting in the way is us. And the way we do that is by being consumed with distractions.

We live in a world of constant noise. We are bombarded on multiple fronts daily, and even think of it as normal now to concentrate on several things at one time. I'm old enough to remember when the network morning news programs first started running news tickers or script along the bottom of the screen. I found it so distracting. Now I don't even notice it, and even ads have been added on the side. We text while we are already talking to someone, listen to books or podcasts while we work, and watch social media while we eat. Rarely are we fully invested in what we are doing. While this may be viewed as productive, it is definitely a compromised effort, and it doesn't begin to work for quiet time with the Lord.

Look, it's totally okay to have fun, give gifts, deck the halls, eat way too many sweets, all the things! That's how we celebrate in our culture, and there's nothing wrong with enjoying the season. But we have to be intentional about keeping the main thing the main thing. Because if we don't, we'll keep missing out on the kind of Christmas our hearts are craving.

To avoid a Martha tilt? Jesus has to come first.
To avoid exhaustion? Jesus has to come first.
To hold onto your joy? Yep, Jesus has to come first.

It's really no different than any other time of the year, but the distractions in December are louder and shinier, aren't they?

Again, I'm not saying don't have fun, please do! Enjoy your traditions. I'm a big fan of the way they create unity, laughter, and lasting memories for our families. But don't become a slave to them. That's when things shift, and suddenly we're serving the season instead of the Savior. Be mindful of what you start, and be honest about when it's time to let something go. We change, and our families change through the years. Traditions can be a beautiful part of Christmas, as long as they stay in their proper place and serve us, not the other way around.

Wow, this is a lot to think about. We've named some more of the idols we face today, and that's not easy. It hits close to home. But it's so worth sitting with, because it can help us see what tempts or attracts us away from Christ. Remember, our goal here is to celebrate Christmas with greater joy. Serving and worshiping from a place of joy. It's not to make it seem doomed with distractions. But as we mentioned earlier, in order to be ready when the season begins, we have to be prepared. Dealing with this now will lead us to a much more joyful Christmas. Sometimes it's not just about starting earlier, it's about starting wiser. How do we do it? Stay tuned. For now, though, let's take a breath and circle back to Santa for a minute to think about what role we want him to play in our Christmas celebrations.

Still with me? Let's pour another cup, maybe decaf this time?

Ponderings 

- Have you ever thought that you put idols before the Lord?
- What role does social media play in your preparations for Christmas?
- What have been some "costs" you have paid for being overly busy at Christmas?

Is your family's holiday more of a celebration of the season or the Savior?

CHAPTER TEN

To Santa or Not to Santa

I mentioned Santa a few pages back and actually want to talk a little more about the famous jolly man. I know Christian families have different takes on the whole Santa thing, and that's okay. Christmas can still be meaningful, joy-filled, and totally centered on Jesus, whether Santa comes down your chimney or not.

For some families, leaving Santa out of the picture helps keep the focus exactly where they want it, on the birth of Christ. It also means not having to explain later why a story they told their kids for years isn't true. That clarity matters to a lot of parents, and I completely get that.

Other families include Santa as more of a fun tradition, not a spiritual one. For them, it's a little extra holiday wonder, not a replacement for the real meaning. They're intentional about keeping Jesus front and center while still enjoying the lighthearted fun that Santa can bring. There's grace for both of these approaches.

What undoubtedly matters is whether we can stay focused on the One that Christmas is truly about. As you read earlier, my children gave equal billing to Santa and Jesus when they were young. And honestly, it's completely natural for young kids to get more excited about Santa. He's got the suit, the sleigh, and the presents, after all. But as they grow and their faith grows, so does their understanding. Over time, they begin to see the difference between a fun, jolly Santa tradition and a heartfelt, joyful celebration of Jesus. Jesus becomes more than just part of the story. He becomes the center of it. Of course, we as parents have to guide them along this faith walk. But, this same focus issue is also a question for you and me. Can we incorporate Santa without slipping into a Martha tilt? Do we strive for the jolly instead of living in the joy of the season? A lot of the Santa stuff can be done ahead of time, which definitely helps. But there can still be some challenges.

One challenge comes when you have little ones who can't quite decide what they want until the last minute. Or they keep changing their minds every other day! That's when Martha might get a little anxious and distracted. Then there's also the eagerly anticipated Christmas morning reveal. The scene you so carefully orchestrated the night before for maximum visual impact. Then, on Christmas morning, your child runs in, full of excitement, and sees the perfectly placed, new shiny blue bike. Instead of jumping up and down and squealing with excitement, he gets quiet because it's not the exact color he was hoping for. Yep, joy doesn't always come where we expect to find it. Of course, this usually gets resolved pretty quickly once the wheels start turning and he realizes he loves it anyway.

Still, let's be honest, it's a bit of an emotional rollercoaster and can put us off balance into a Martha tilt. My point is, even the fun stuff can rob us of joy if we let it. Of course, with Santa comes stockings. This is definitely a situation where size matters. My mom always did a great job of providing us with a beautifully simple yet festive Christmas. Our stockings were not large, but held enough. And, thanks to Mary Poppins, we all know: "Enough is as good as a feast". Bob's family, however, had these huge knit stockings, and the minute I saw them, I was a fan. So, which do you think I selected for our kids? Yep, the big knit ones, which of course I spent hours knitting myself. And for years now, I've spent months finding enough "stuff" to fill them!

Once again, it all comes back to where our hearts are anchored. Santa can absolutely be part of the fun, but Jesus has to remain first. If we stay in a Mary posture, the extra drama and effort Santa sometimes brings doesn't have to be an issue. It is a personal call, a choice. We will be talking about choices later, but as far as Santa goes, there really is no wrong answer.

Now, with all that said, let me share a little about our own Christmas Eve tradition. Christmas Eve at our house, like most aspects of our holiday, has always been an event. It's Bob's and my favorite day of the year. What started years ago at a dear friend's home eventually moved to our place after they, sadly for us, relocated to Memphis. A handful of families would gather, arms full of yummy casseroles, with sugar-crazed toddlers and fussy, sleepy babies in tow. We'd share a quick dinner, raise a quick toast, and then brace ourselves for the not-so-quick evening ahead. And yes, I have overused the word quick! Because that's exactly what it was, a fast kickoff to a night that usually required assembly of something that was not quick or fast in any way, shape, or form.

Over the years, the gathering grew as we welcomed more families into the mix. We had our regular core group, but others came and went, depending on whether they had family in town or just needed a place to land on Christmas Eve. Naturally, I had to take it up a notch, because holiday magic doesn't just make itself, right? So somewhere between dinner and dessert (which of course had now evolved into a full seated meal for 20–30 people), Bob would develop a mysterious headache and disappear.

Tragically, he always seemed to miss Santa's visit. I surely do hate that for him. All of a sudden, there would be a loud "HO! HO! HO!", and all the kids would get excited because Santa had stopped by. When the kids were little, they'd each get their moment on Santa's lap for a quick conversation, a reminder of whose birthday we were celebrating, and a gift. It was always sweet and hilarious hearing what they'd share. My sons, Bo and Mac, each spent a couple of their younger years dressed up as Santa's elf and proudly helped Santa distribute gifts. It undoubtedly was a special time.

As all the kids got older, Santa took a more streamlined approach and simply handed out presents like a pro. He never stayed long, busy night and all, but he usually managed to step outside and wave down a few passing cars, much to the delight of the neighborhood. Eventually, guests would head home, though not before the adults enjoyed a little holiday cheer ourselves and sang our traditional song. For years, when everyone had left, we would all get comfy and shift gears into observing our own family traditions. For us, that meant scattering reindeer food in the yard, writing letters to Santa, setting out cookies with milk, and curling up by the fire for a reading of *'Twas the Night Before Christmas.*

Then, and it was usually pretty late, it was time for our kids to go to bed... and the start of a long night for the now miraculously recovered Bob (from earlier headache) and me. As the kids got older, though, we would clean quickly and have a quick turnaround to be at the 11:00 P.M. Christmas Eve service. We still had major clean-up ahead before we could even think about prepping for the morning. Obviously, our guests had pitched in earlier and helped with the initial pickup before they left. But as you can imagine, we were still usually up until the wee hours, running on fumes and munching on leftovers from the evening.

Now, at this point, we could pause and have a heyday analyzing my compulsion to make everything absolutely perfect for this night. If it wasn't clear before why I'm right here with you in the struggle, I'm sure it is now. Total focus on perfection. For years, I went all out, pulling out the stemware, the china, the silver, the chargers, the cloth napkins... all of it. Each table was fully decorated, complete with place cards and little favors at each seat. I think there were a few times I gave in and used paper plates for our younger guests, but overall, no shortcuts were taken. I was determined to make it magical and special, even if it totally exhausted me in the process! Which it usually did!

But the truth is, I absolutely loved hosting this event. These friends who joined us were like family, and we all enjoyed being together. I always felt that it was my gift to them to create this special evening, and they genuinely seemed to look forward to coming each year. It was fun, festive, and Christ was definitely present in many ways. I even felt momentarily energized by the Christian fellowship with dear friends and my family. Think about it, by the time Christmas Eve rolled around, everything that was going to get done had either been done or just wasn't happening. And honestly, there was a strange peace in that. A surrender, even. The stillness begins to settle in, but it's following weeks of busy days and stacks of to-do lists. It's as if joy and weariness are holding hands.

Yet, as we have been discussing, even when we're doing things we love, like shopping, decorating, planning meals, and setting the table, we still get tired. But here's the thing with Christmas. It's not just a day or two of extra effort. It's weeks of keeping up that same energy level, on top of everything else, daily, that's already going on. This is the combustible combination that I mentioned earlier. The season is full of so many good things that we can easily leave out the best thing of all. That's when the joy starts to wear thin, and the exhaustion starts to settle in. That's when we don't get the Christmas we long for. And that's exactly why we need a deeper, lasting kind of joy, the kind that only the Lord can give. It's being connected to Him that keeps us full of His joy, even when the details of the day are many.

I wasn't starting at Jesus' feet. I wasn't taking the time to sit with Him before I was taking on the exciting tasks of the day. My inner peace and joy were depleted even though I was doing what I loved. Our activities, no matter how fun or service-oriented they are, can make us happy, but they can not give us the joy that lasts. Only Jesus can. Further, we are never called to serve the Lord without first being with Him and experiencing all He has for us. This allows us to live from a place of fullness. That's what the Lord was telling

Martha. Being with Him must come first, before the needs of the day are addressed. Only then can we have the joy that is contagious to others as we serve, and only then can we recognize and resist the distractions around us.

Another part of our Christmas Eve was that we always had a birthday cake for Jesus, and the kids all sang to Him before they dove in. It was a simple moment, but one that helped anchor the night in a meaningful way, even amid the familiar chaos of kids everywhere! I must also mention that before any of the dinner festivities even kicked off, Bob would read from Luke's Gospel, reminding us all why we were gathered in the first place. We would gather in a circle, and then he'd read and pray. And I mean pray. How long were his prayers, you ask? Let's just say they were long enough for us to start side-glancing at each other, heads tilted, giggles suppressed, looking at our watches. Because if you'd ever heard Bob pray on Christmas Eve, you knew it was going long and you needed to find my son Mac when you arrived to place your friendly wager on the over/under for how many minutes Bob would go. For years, Bob had no idea we were doing this, and it made it all the more fun. Now, looking back, even the length of those prayers somehow became part of the tradition.

So, Santa has worked for us. As our kids were growing up and we were trying to teach them what it means to follow Jesus, it often felt like we were saying "no" to a lot of things they wanted to do. But Santa was something we felt we could say "yes" to and still keep our focus on Christ. Following Jesus is already so countercultural, and that can be especially hard when you're young. Including Santa gave our kids a way to participate in something fun and widely shared. For us, it was a little piece of holiday culture we could enjoy without compromising what mattered most.

One other thing to note, like most things, this Christmas Eve tradition had its season, and as our core group all started having grandchildren, it began to get a little complicated. Now, when my kids bring their families home for Christmas, we all want to enjoy just being with each other. I find I want to spend my time differently now, much more focused on my grandchildren. Taking the time to see Christmas through their young eyes while sharing some insight through mine. Never be hesitant when you feel a tradition is coming to a natural end. Life has seasons and rhythms for a reason. God created order when He created the heavens and the earth. Our lives have seasons, and our traditions can too. We will talk about this some more in a minute.

All this Santa talk is making me think about hot chocolate. You? Grab what you need and hurry back. Santa is here...

Ponderings 

- Do you experience more happiness or joy during the Christmas Season? What is the difference?

- What would it look like to spend more time with Jesus at the beginning of your day?

- Is it hard for you to settle for less than perfect during the long Christmas Season? What is the source of this pressure?

CHAPTER ELEVEN

Suit Up: Dressed To Impress

Are you ready for something new? Now, just for fun and hopefully to give you a little encouragement for the festivities ahead, we're going to talk about Santa's big red suit. Not because we're focusing on him by any means, but because I think it might actually serve as a surprisingly helpful visual. I know this is a stretch, but I'm hoping that sometime during the Christmas season, this will perhaps provide you a giggle or, preferably, remind you visually not only of your spiritual strength, but also its source. Everything we've talked about so far points to one simple truth: keeping our eyes fixed on Jesus is the key to maintaining the strength we need. The strength we need to fuel our inner joy as well as to avoid being pulled away by all the other shiny, glittery distractions that pop up everywhere during this season. It's what Mary was able to do. Choosing to sit at Jesus' feet kept her totally connected to Him and not distracted by all that indeed needed to be done. For Mary, those needs came next after her time with the Lord. Martha did serve well, but at the expense of being with Jesus first. When we fail to prioritize being at His feet before anything else, we eventually slip off track and tilt to a more Martha experience. We can't sit at Jesus' feet all day, and that is not what Jesus is saying here. But we must choose to place ourselves there before we go about our day, even if the day consists solely of Christian service. We must precede our days with prayer. Only then can we maintain our joy and recognize if our other activities are becoming idols. Again, Martha wasn't wrong to be serving. Jesus never scolded her for that. But He did point out that Mary had chosen what was better. Martha got pulled away from Jesus by things that looked important. And wow, isn't that the whole Christmas struggle? Everything seems important!

We think we are "all good". We love Jesus, and we certainly know it's His birthday. Our nativity is set up at home, and we have it all under control. But this assumption can be sneaky. It lulls us into thinking we are spiritually on track, even while we're running ourselves ragged. You already know that this always catches up with us. We notice that our joy has disappeared and stress has taken its place. In other words, we realize we are disconnected from our Savior and have allowed His presence to be replaced.

So this is where Santa's suit comes in. I know it's a bit of a stretch... but honestly, I think it works. You're going to see Santa everywhere this time of year, whether he visits your house or not. He's on mugs, in commercials, on wrapping paper, and on yard inflatables two stories tall. So why not let that red suit remind us of something deeper, something real? Like the armor of God. Now stay with me. This is not to be disrespectful, but to provide a reminder to you during the season to stay grounded, strong, and centered in Christ when the season gets crazy. Hey, we need things to remind us to stay focused on what's important, and I'm not above repurposing a little holiday imagery. You know how Santa never leaves the North Pole without his full red suit? Boots, belt, coat, hat, the whole thing. It's part of who he is, and he doesn't take off without it. In a way, we're not so different. We've got something to wear too, but it's not red, festive, or fuzzy. It is, however, powerful and protective. It's the armor of God.

> Finally, be strong in the Lord, and in the strength of His might. Put on the full armor of God, that you may be able to stand firm against the schemes of the devil. For our struggle is not against flesh and blood, but against the rulers, against the powers, against the world forces of this darkness, against the spiritual forces of wickedness in the heavenly places. Therefore, take up the full armor of God, that you may be able to resist in the evil day, and having done everything, to stand firm. Stand firm therefore, having girded your loins with truth, and having put on the breastplate of righteousness, and having shod your feet with the preparation of the gospel of peace; in addition to all, taking up the shield of faith with which you will be able to extinguish all the flaming missiles of the evil one. And take the helmet of salvation, and the sword of the Spirit, which is the word of God. With all prayer and petition pray at all times in the Spirit, and with this in view, be on the alert with all perseverance and petition for all the saints. (Ephesians 6:10–18)

First, a brief reminder of our armor. In Ephesians 6, Paul tells us to put on the full armor of God. He explains that this is where our strength comes from for spiritual battles. This strength allows us to stand firm against evil. We've already agreed that Christmas can indeed be a battle itself. During this season, there is a very active challenge going on for our attention. Right? There's a tension during the season, where culture pulls us one way, and Christ calls us another. This is no accident and has proven to be an effective tactic to pull us away from Christ. The enemy would love nothing more than to use this season to derail our joy and steal our attention. So yes, this armor we've been talking about, it matters. It helps us stay grounded when the season gets loud, overwhelming, or just plain exhausting. It's how we walk in peace, stand in truth, and hang onto joy when everything else is pulling at us. Take the time to reread Ephesians 6 to reacquaint yourself with our true armor and its power as Paul explains it.

Now, just for fun, and because you're going to see him everywhere, from coffee mugs to front lawns, let's talk about Santa for a second. He never leaves the North Pole without his red suit on, right? It's his uniform, his gear. It's how he shows up ready for his job. OK, now here's the "stretch". When you notice him this year, let his work outfit be a reminder to you of what you can wear spiritually to equip you for your work at Christmas, also. Here's a quick look:

Belt of Truth – Santa's belt is for show. Ours keeps us grounded in what's real: Christmas is about Jesus, not perfection.

Breastplate of Righteousness – Let Santa's big red coat remind you that you are covered in grace. Snuggle into that!

Shoes of Peace – He's got boots. We've got peace that carries us through the chaos, stores, schedules, menus, and all.

Shield of Faith – Santa carries a sack of toys to bring fun gifts and joy to children. We carry the shield of faith to protect us when darts of doubt and lies come our way to steal our joy.

Helmet of Salvation – Santa wears an iconic hat. We get something much better, though. Truth that protects our thoughts and keeps us steady. Don't believe the lies of the enemy or give value to cries for worldly perfection.

Sword of the Spirit – Santa carries and checks his list to complete his job. We carry God's Word, and it's powerful. When we feel overwhelmed, it reminds us of what's true.

So this Christmas, don't just power through. Don't get stuck worrying about many things. You don't have to earn your peace or perfect your way into joy. Because that's not even possible, just suit up in what's already yours: truth, righteousness, peace, faith, salvation, and the Word. Your God hasn't left you unequipped. He's given you everything you need to stand, not strive. When you see a Santa, let it remind you of how you are equipped to do your work, also. Not only does Jesus equip us to stand firm amidst all the tempting distractions of the season, He is also our good Shepherd who will guide us personally through it all. So as we leave the Santa scene behind, we are going to focus on the power resulting from and the commitment needed to experience a Mary Christmas. And then, I can't wait to talk about the shepherds!

So take a breath. Hopefully, you're still enjoying your tea. Curl up in the quiet (even if it's just five minutes), and remember that the battle is real, but so is your armor. Suit up! You've got this, we've got this, because He's got us, Jesus that is, not Santa.

Santa talk makes me think of Christmas cookies. Cookies with your tea, anyone?

Ponderings 

- How can you stop chasing perfection and instead pursue the Prince of Peace?

- How does the enemy try to steal your joy?

- Which piece of the armor would be most helpful to you during this season?

- Do you think that when you see a Santa, you can think about your armor? (Hope so!)

Part Three

Mary Has Chosen

> Remain in Me, and I in you. Just as the branch cannot bear fruit of itself but must remain in the vine, so neither can you unless you remain in Me. I am the vine, you are the branches; the one who remains in Me, and I in him bears much fruit, for apart from Me you can do nothing. — John 15:4-5

Faith is stronger than the frenzy, but we have to stay connected.

CHAPTER TWELVE

The Power of a Wise Yes

Throughout my 30s, I was often encouraged to learn how to say "no". Have you heard this also? No to commitments I didn't have time for and no to things that didn't entirely interest me. It was all about setting boundaries and not stretching myself too thin. On the surface, it seemed like good advice.

But as I've grown older and stepped out on some cliffs involving some big decisions with the Lord, I've learned that making a good choice is much more about saying a wise yes. It's a simple yet powerful shift in perspective! Setting boundaries matters, but what's even more important is aligning our yeses with God's plan. Saying no is often about self-preservation, but saying the right yes? That's about stepping into obedience, purpose, and the abundant life He's specifically ordained for you. It's aligning your path and plan with His purpose. It's about yielding control. And truthfully, it's a far less stressful, far more fulfilling, and even more exciting way to live.

So, what does this have to do with Christmas and idols?

Once I realized that idols don't have to look like golden statues and that they can be anything I've made too important in my heart, I suddenly saw that they were hiding in plain sight, especially around Christmas. The season has a way of turning up the volume on everything, trying to steal my focus. The pressure to make everything magical, the drive to get it all just right, and the fear of letting people down can consume me. If I'm not paying attention, those things quietly start taking center stage. And the most challenging part is that I'm creating these pressures myself. Sure, culture is pointing me in their direction, but I am much too easy a target. That's why I know I need to head into the Christmas game ready. And by that I mean spiritually ready. I'm talking heart-guarded, eyes-on-Jesus kind of ready. Because when everything's calling for my attention, I want to stay focused on the One who truly matters.

So, while it's been fun (and maybe a little therapeutic) to vent about holiday frustrations and to talk about all the distractions, I want us to shift our focus. Because deep down, I don't think any of us want to just survive Christmas in a flurry of busyness with maybe a couple of emotional breakdowns thrown in. What we honestly want is a Christmas that fills us. A celebration that doesn't just look magical for everyone else, but that can genuinely restore you and me in the process. But somewhere between the Elf on the Shelf daily drama and managing package deliveries without the dogs getting out, we lose sight of the One we're supposed to be celebrating. So, our next step after identifying the idols that steal our attention away from a meaningful Christmas is concentrating on saying a strong, committed YES to putting Jesus first.

Some aspects of Christmas we can't control, like holiday traffic, holiday crowds, and unexpected mishaps. But if we step into Christmas with a strong "yes" to walking closely with Jesus and we commit to daily renewing ourselves in Him, distractions and frustrations lose their power and grip. Joy wins. Such a choice sets us on a path of walking with Him and spending time with Him. This decision can be hard to prioritize anytime, but during the holidays, it can not only seem impossible, but it can also appear as just another thing to do, and sadly, lose its appeal.

Isn't it ironic that a season that's supposed to be all about joy can leave us feeling anything but joyful? As Christian women and moms, we step into Christmas wanting to make it meaningful. Keeping up traditions, creating special moments, and making sure everyone around us feels seen and loved. The world tells us that joy comes from such efforts, but deep down, we know better. Real joy, the perfect and defiant joy which can not be taken from us, only comes from one source, Jesus. But having lived through many holiday seasons, I have learned that peace and fulfillment come from not just saying yes to following Jesus, but also abiding in Him daily. There is absolutely no other way to renew my yes and continually sustain my joy. Why is this so easy to say yet so much harder to put into practice? For years, I thought I could produce joy for everyone around me, and I tried so hard to do it. But not only is that just not how it works, it deprives my family and friends of seeking and finding the true source of joy themselves. If I am not my own source of joy, how can I expect to be theirs? It's simple. I can't, and you can't either.

Scripture tells us that true joy not only comes from the Lord, but that He even wants us to experience the exact same joy He has! His joy isn't scarce or temporary. Even better, the capacity for this joy is already in us, and His desire is for it to overflow in our lives (John 15:11)! Did you catch that? His joy is already in you, and He wants it to overflow! There's no magical five-step process to obtain joy. Jesus is telling us it is ours already. Think about that for a minute, though. If only Jesus can supply our joy, then we must stay close to Him for it to be refilled. This joy doesn't leave us and hides at Christmas. We leave. We run and search everywhere else when, in fact, we need to be sitting and looking within and seeking the Lord.

Choices can be difficult. Choosing to slow down at Christmas isn't easy. The world is whirling around you, full of enticing distractions. It's a continual choice and a hard one. To make our commitment stick, we have to fully believe not only in the why of our decision (seeking the Christmas joy we have been missing) but, most importantly, we have to be fully committed to the WHO (Jesus) of our decision.

That's why this year, I'm thinking less about perfect plans and more about purposeful yeses. Saying no to the chaos is great, but even better? Saying yes to what draws us closer to Christ. Yes to slow mornings (even if it's just five sacred minutes) with coffee or tea and quiet. Yes to moments of connection with our children, not just corralling them from one activity to another. Yes to worship that re-centers our hearts when everything feels off-kilter. Yes to peace over scrolling through Pinterest. And to you moms with babies and toddlers, we all know how beautiful and busy those years are. But figure out a way to schedule some time for you with the Lord, even if you're not alone. Bring Him into what you are doing and listen for His voice.

Let's say yes to less stressing and more resting in Him. Let's say yes like Mary. We hear a lot about starting early to get ready for Christmas in order to make the season less stressful. This implies we should organize our "to-dos" so we can get more done. The better, more "Mary" choice would be to start wiser and be better prepared to resist the stressful aspects of the season.

We will start talking about Mary and her choice in the next chapter. Her yes was powerful and still witnesses to us today. Like Mary, when our yeses are intentionally rooted in what matters, the season shifts. It stops feeling like something we have to hold together and starts feeling like the gift it was meant to be. And think about it, Jesus never asked us to host the perfect Christmas. He just wants our hearts. That's what's on His Christmas list.

It's that time again! Let's heat another pot of tea. Please don't say you've had enough! Never! Snuggle in. We're getting closer to the best part, the part where we say a strong yes to that which can't be taken from us. Top off your cup because this next part is worth savoring.

Ponderings 

- Can you think of times in your life when you have said a strong yes to something?

- Where do you tend to search for joy?

- Right now, before Christmas activities get started, can you think of a time you can schedule daily to be with the Lord and commit to it with a strong yes?

CHAPTER THIRTEEN

Mary's Choice, Our Decision

Don't we all want to say yes like Mary did? In our Scripture, Mary chose Jesus before anything else, even the urgent pressing things right in front of her. She left her sister to handle the hosting responsibilities and sat at Jesus' feet instead. We don't get the impression that it was a particularly hard choice for her either. When challenged, Jesus also quickly and fully affirmed her choice as the best one. Maybe Mary was just wired that way, more naturally drawn to worship and learning. Sitting still with Jesus felt right to her. Meanwhile, Martha was wired differently. She leaned toward serving, making sure everyone was cared for and everything was done.

So where do you fall? Is saying yes to Jesus first each day a struggle, or does it sound amazing? Maybe a little of both? Sometimes we think we're doing well spending time with the Lord, but when Christmas rolls around, it's suddenly harder than we expected. And it doesn't seem to matter how many years we've tried to get it right. We end up feeling frantic instead of focused.

The truth is, when we start each day aligned with the Lord, we can trust we're exactly where He wants us to be. That's the kind of steady guidance we need to make it through the holiday rush. God doesn't usually hand us a full-season game plan. Instead, He invites us to follow Him step by step, day by day. And even then, it's still tough not to fall headfirst into Martha's version of Christmas. You know, the one that doesn't satisfy, full of hustle, lists, and yuletide overload.

The whole pivot from Mary to Martha is really about a shift in priorities. It can be a quiet rearranging of the heart where something else slowly begins to take the place of Jesus. Or, it can be a bold choice based on the feeling that you've got everything under control. You feel confident that you can handle our culture's seasonal demands first and still be able to spend time with Jesus later. Whichever it is, that shift can happen quickly, this time of year. We are bombarded with so many good choices to make that the best choice will get lost if we don't stay focused. Because if we don't stay focused, we slip into our old patterns that we are trying to avoid.

Face it, there's always work to do, meals to cook, and tasks to complete. But these things should always come after spending time with the Lord. Everything should begin at His feet. Otherwise, it can not be sustained. This time with Him allows us to work from a position of joy. This time with Him recenters us on what is important. Done correctly, this priority choice reflects the better pivot, from Martha to Mary. We need time with Jesus to be renewed, to be filled again, so we can walk through each day of this season with joy and stay grounded in what matters. Christmas is not a short sprint. It is at least a month of enduring our culture screaming that you should do more, and be more, in order to perfect your family's holiday. In other words, to make it magical. Without this time with the Lord daily, we're quickly running on empty, trying to pour from a cup that was never meant to stay full on its own. Along with this depletion, the strength of our yes wilts. The noise of the world will have our attention.

We are so blessed to have a Good Shepherd to pull us back onto the path.

I can't think about Christmas without mentioning shepherds. We know our Good Shepherd is infinitely able to care for His sheep. Especially when we go astray. And oh boy, do we like sheep go astray, especially at Christmas.

Like sheep, we wander off. We head straight towards the cliff of busyness, the rushing waters of unrealistic expectations, and the thorns of high-performance standards. We chase all the wrong things when the one thing we need most is what we have mistakenly run from, our Shepherd. He is waiting for us to be still and choose the better portion. Good thing he is also patient.

And here's the beauty of that better portion: we're not just sitting still for the sake of silence or rest. We are actively receiving something we desperately need: the joy and peace of the Lord. We can't pull up to a gas pump and sit there expecting to fill up our tank. We have to connect our tank with the hose running to the pump. That's the kind of connection we need with the Lord, directly from Him to us. This is the only way we can fill up and strengthen ourselves from the inside out. The kind of strength that doesn't crumble under unmet expectations, hectic family gatherings, or a burned batch of sugar cookies. It's the joy that becomes our strength (Nehemiah 8:10), and the peace that guards our hearts and minds in Christ Jesus (Philippians 4:7).

So scripture is telling us that not only do we receive this wonderful joy from our Shepherd, but that He also brings us peace. This peace, like our joy, cannot be taken from us. The Bible calls it the peace that passes understanding. Joy brings strength. Peace protects our heart.

I want to pause here to stress a point that has meant a great deal to me and made a big difference in my relationship with the Lord. Our connection with the Lord needs to be direct, like the hose at the gas pump. Mary got this and sat directly at the Lord's feet and listened directly as He taught. She was connected. This was and is such a privilege and should not be taken for granted or undervalued. Back in the Old Testament days, direct access to God wasn't even an option for most people. Honestly, they believed that if they saw God directly, they'd drop dead! So instead, God used Moses with the Ten Commandments, or spoke to the Israelites through prophets to deliver His messages. Only a chosen few heard directly from God Himself.

Today, though, because of Jesus' sacrificial death on the cross, we have a direct line straight to God all the time. This is our gift as His children. Incredibly, though, so many of us don't take advantage of this divine access. Instead, we seek easier, quicker answers through people whose faith we respect and admire. Whether a pastor, a teacher, a speaker, a book, or a podcast, we rely on others for the answers we are seeking. And sure, these people and things can be instructive and encouraging, but they're still secondhand. Their role is to direct us to the Lord. But nothing beats hearing directly from God Himself, speaking exactly what He wants you, personally, to know. It's the difference between a fast food diet faith and a deeply nourished faith. Martha probably figured someone would tell her what Jesus said, but that would not be the same as hearing for herself. Plus, she would only hear what the other person had been touched by. Yes, hearing the Lord takes time, but it is not wasted time; it's your own personal divine appointment. It's you talking to the creator of the universe! The bond developed between you and the Lord will be much stronger, deeper, and more personal.

This type of relationship is what Mary chose by sitting at Jesus' feet. This should be our yes, indeed, our very confident yes. This is the one thing. This is the answer. This is the choice. Abiding in Christ. Deep down, you've known it all along. What else could it be? But this is so much easier said than done, or so many of us wouldn't struggle. The minute you want to spend time with the Lord, the enemy will all of a sudden give you a compulsion to get something done...even to take care of the ironing you've avoided for months. Has this happened to you? And at Christmas, the distractions at his disposal are much more tempting than ironing.

Resist it. Remember the strength of your Yes. Remember what you are saying yes to. And remember what Jesus said to Martha about Mary's yes. He said Mary "has chosen the good part, which shall not be taken from her" (Luke 10:42). That's what He offers us still today. A deeply rooted, Spirit-given strength not to just survive Christmas or any time, but to live it well. By saying yes to remaining in His presence, or abiding, He promises we will not lose Him, His peace, or His joy. Instead of running ourselves ragged trying to create the perfect holiday, we can experience a genuinely meaningful

Christmas by simply resting in Him. Then, when it comes to all the seasonal to-dos, we'll find that what we choose to do naturally flows out of gratitude for what Jesus has already done for us. We will be working from a place of joy. A very different mindset than trying to match a Pinterest setting or have the latest greatest Instagram decorations.

Are you with me? Are you skeptical? Do you feel like that is so easy to say, but so hard to commit to in real life with messy houses, hungry families, and a mountain of laundry? How can we possibly choose to abide when there is so much to be done? How can we stay at the gas pump when we need to hit the road? Jesus isn't saying we need to sit at His feet all day. He is telling us that everything should begin there. Whether it is service (like Martha was providing) or worship (like Mary was enjoying). Scripture shows us that He prefers to guide us one day at a time, like the shepherd guiding and protecting his sheep. He is near and isn't going anywhere. He is a faithful, good shepherd, and as you practice being in His presence, you will learn to trust Him more and more. This will flow from you experiencing His faithfulness firsthand. Are you starting to get a glimpse of how meaningful your Christmas could be?

We aren't done yet, and the best part is Jesus is never done pursuing us and showing us the way to live. It's what we thankfully celebrate at Christmas. He knows our pain. He sees our struggle. He's been here too. In fact, let's go back to our Lord's arrival on that not-so-silent night.

If you didn't top off your tea a minute ago, you might want to top it off now because we're headed where it's dry, dark, and smelly...

Ponderings 

- When you sit with the Lord, are you actively trying to hear Him? Resting in Him? Are you talking the whole time?

- Have you ever felt or heard the Lord speak to you?

- How would your Christmas change if you, like Mary, said a strong yes to Jesus and practiced being in His presence daily? What would be the hardest part for you?

CHAPTER FOURTEEN
Calling All Shepherds

In the same region there were some shepherds staying out in the fields and keeping watch over their flock by night. And an angel of the Lord suddenly stood before them, and the glory of the Lord shone around them; and they were terribly frightened. And the angel said to them, "Do not be afraid; for behold, I bring you good news of a great joy which shall be for all the people; for today in the city of David there has been born for you a Savior, who is Christ the Lord. And this will be a sign for you: you will find a baby wrapped in cloths, and lying in a manger." And suddenly there appeared with the angel a multitude of the heavenly host praising God and saying, "Glory to God in the highest, And on earth peace among men with whom He is pleased." And it came about when the angels had gone away from them into heaven, that the shepherds began saying to one another, "Let us go straight to Bethlehem then, and see this thing that has happened which the Lord has made known to us." And they came in haste and found their way to Mary and Joseph, and the baby as He lay in the manger. And when they had seen this, they made known the statement which had been told them about this Child. And all who heard it wondered at the things which were told them by the shepherds. But Mary treasured up all these things, pondering them in her heart. And the shepherds went back, glorifying and praising God for all that they had heard and seen, just as had been told them. (Luke 2:8–20)

Linger a moment and read this very familiar scripture carefully. Did you catch it? "Good news of a great JOY which will be for all the people"… that's you and me! Choosing this joy is a strong YES from me. It's what Mary chose, also.

One of the most joyful parts of our family's Christmas when the kids were little was our church's Christmas pageant. The youngest participants were angels and shepherds, and there were a lot of them. I had an angel and two shepherds in the mix, and somehow every year when the pageant began, I felt like Christmas had officially arrived. As the music began and the lights dimmed, you could hear the noise of the young cast waiting in the hall to enter. With halos slightly askew and headdresses slipping, they marched in wide-eyed with a burst of noise and enthusiasm. The excitement among these little shepherds and angels was contagious. And honestly, their unfiltered joy was exactly what we as parents needed after all the preparations.

Surely, the multitude of angels singing and praising God that first Christmas night is reflected in the joy and excitement of these little angels now. And I imagine the shepherds racing to find baby Jesus were probably a pretty noisy bunch too! I picture them talking over each other, hurrying along, maybe even tripping in their excitement, just like some little shepherds I know.

That holy night was anything but quiet. It was bursting with wonder, awe, and celebration. The angels proclaimed Christ's birth with the enthusiasm of fully understanding the magnitude of what had just happened. And in Bethlehem, the shepherds found so much more than a baby in a manger. They met the King whom they and their people had been waiting for. The one who would guide them, care for them, and protect them...just like a shepherd.

Much has been written about why God chose to reveal Jesus' birth to the shepherds first. As you may know, shepherds weren't exactly at the top of the social ladder 2,000 years ago. Their work with sheep made them "unclean" by religious standards, and most people looked down on them. But God doesn't do things by accident, and it was no mistake that these humble, often-overlooked workers were the first to hear the news.

Think about it, God wraps the ultimate gift and delivers it to the least likely address. The King of kings shows up in a feed trough, and the VIP guest list starts with night-shift shepherds who still smell like campfire and sheep. Talk about flipping expectations! In that moment, heaven basically whispers, "Hey, nobody's too small, messy, or overlooked for My love." If divine glory can light up a drafty cave, it can absolutely sparkle in our comfortable living rooms as well as in our worn-out hearts. Do you sometimes feel like you are the least likely person God would show up for? The least likely address? The Bible assures us there is no such person or place! Jesus first appeared to the shepherds, the least of these, the absolute bottom in that culture's society. They got the front row seats and the breaking news release. God loves all His children, including you and me, and offers us a front row seat daily to sit with and walk with Him.

The birth of Jesus wasn't staged to impress; it was designed to invite. God didn't wait for perfect conditions, polished people, or Instagram-worthy surroundings. He chose a dirty, messy manger on purpose. It's like He was saying, "Don't wait until everything looks just right, just come." Just like Mary (Martha's sister), chose the important over the urgent. We can choose the same. We can say yes to that which can't be taken away. Yes to Jesus' presence. Even better, yes to realizing His presence and His peace, in spite of all the urgent tasks of the season.

And if that's how God chose to introduce His Son, maybe we can stop striving for the flawless version of Christmas ourselves. We can shake up the cultural script that says it has to be big, busy, and beautiful to be meaningful because our God isn't looking for perfection. He's looking for presence. Not perfect table settings, but hearts that are set on Him. Like Mary's.

So this year, as you are placing your shepherds in the nativity or dressing your little shepherds for a pageant, pause and remember what a powerful yet simple announcement God gave the world that first Christmas. Presenting His Son, our Good Shepherd, to the lowly, dirty shepherds from the field, whose vocation still today helps us understand the depth to which our Savior loves us. And listen for the joy that still echoes in every child who throws on a halo or a shepherd's robe, eager to be a part of the greatest story ever told and the greatest event that ever happened.

The utter simplicity of this royal birth adds to the power of God's message. Perhaps a more simplified celebration in our homes would also have a powerful impact on others? Perhaps it would have a kingdom impact on ourselves. Either way, it would reflect Mary's choice of abiding in Christ and offer us access to the joy we crave.

The words joy and abiding make me think of wrapping my hands around a warm mug of tea! Do you need a refill? I'd love to linger a little longer with the shepherds. Let's continue our conversation. There is so much we can learn from them.

Ponderings 

- Are there a few changes you could make to your family's Christmas celebration that would greatly simplify the occasion without changing what is traditionally meaningful to you?

- What would it look like for you to be able to abide in the Lord's presence daily during the seasonal rush?

- Do you spend more time attempting to impress others at your celebration or to invite others in? Think about the difference.

- What does "Good news of great joy" mean to you?

CHAPTER FIFTEEN

Following Our Shepherd Through the Holiday Haze

Several years ago, the Lord led me to spend a summer studying Psalm 23. At the time, I wasn't at all sure why, but now, as I sit here writing this book, it all clicks. This Psalm paints such a beautiful, comforting picture of who Jesus is and just how deeply He loves us. It also reminds us that keeping our eyes on Him is the only way to stay on the right path, especially during the busy and often overwhelming Christmas season. If we want the kind of Christmas that feels peaceful, joyful, and maybe even a little fun again, we've got to say yes to staying close to the One who knows us and loves us the best.

Like we've talked about, it's so easy to get off course this time of year. The to-do lists, the expectations, the everything. So, as we take a brief look at Psalm 23, my hope is that it helps us renew our trust in Jesus, grow our love for Him, and strengthen our yes to walking closely, daily, with our Good Shepherd. Now don't worry, I'm not turning this into a deep dive Bible study on Psalm 23. But I once heard someone say that every truth in the New Testament has a picture in the Old Testament, and Psalm 23 is a perfect example. It gives us such a clear picture of not only who God is, but also who He wants to be to us. I just want to pull out three observations that definitely stood out to me. Points that I think will encourage and strengthen us as we say yes (or yes again) to staying close to Him this Christmas. Because honestly, that yes requires a lot of strength, determination, and focus to maintain.

The LORD is my shepherd, I shall not want.

He makes me lie down in green pastures; He leads me beside quiet waters.

He restores my soul; He guides me in the paths of righteousness For His name's sake.

Even though I walk through the valley of the shadow of death, I fear no evil; for Thou art with me; Thy rod and Thy staff, they comfort me.

Thou dost prepare a table before me in the presence of my enemies; Thou hast anointed my head with oil; My cup overflows.

Surely goodness and lovingkindness will follow me all the days of my life, And I will dwell in the house of the LORD forever. (Psalm 23:1–6)

First, when we read this Psalm with a Western perspective, we picture a shepherd placing his sheep in green pastures that are like fields of tall green grass. A beautiful spot where they can feast and rest for weeks safely. But in fact, that is not at all what David is describing here. In the rocky desert terrain of Israel, a green pasture is a mountain that has bite-sized patches of grass growing around clumps of rocks. Sheep have to closely follow their shepherd, who carefully searches for these scattered spots. In addition, these little mouthful bites only last a day in the heat. Amazingly, though, the humidity and moisture off the Mediterranean Sea at night enable more little patches to grow around the rocks and to be food for the next day. Sheep have to depend daily on their shepherd to find not only their next meal, but basically their next mouthful.

Second, the Hebrew word used for *paths* is translated as circular in nature, like a track[4]. But these particular roundabout paths were anything but easy to navigate. Shepherds would lead their sheep in circular, narrow paths around the mountains to get them up and down safely. In Israel, these desert paths are visible from a distance as they are etched in the hills circling around, leading up and down. If a sheep were to try to go straight up or down the hillside, they would fall and probably get stuck. These paths also intersect and can be very confusing to navigate. The only way to ensure the sheep's safety is for them to follow the narrow path, the right path, with their eyes fixed on their shepherd.

Isn't that such a powerful picture? I had read Psalm 23 so many times before, but learning what green pastures and paths looked like in David's world totally shifted things for me. It reminded me that following Jesus isn't about finding one big, perfect pasture and settling in for a lifetime of spiritual ease. It's about trusting Him for just enough for today and then doing it again tomorrow. He's not dropping breadcrumbs or leaving us to figure it out on our own. He's right here, daily leading us to the next patch of grace we didn't even know we needed.

---

4   "Bible Hub. *Strong's Hebrew 4570 – Magal* (מַעְגָּל). Bible Hub, https:// biblehub.com/hebrew/4570.htm. Accessed 16 Aug. 2025."

And those winding paths? They aren't the straight, smooth kind we wish for. So sometimes following Him feels slow, repetitive, and even a little frustrating when we don't see the bigger picture. Don't you sometimes just feel stuck? It's like you're spinning your wheels and going nowhere fast. Yet, He knows exactly where we're going. He also knows how to get us there safely, even when it feels like we're just walking in circles. But wait, who wants to feel like they're going in circles, especially at Christmas! Speed and efficiency are everything, right? This is what makes Mary's choice so hard and counterintuitive. This is the sitting still and dwelling with the Lord, while Martha and the world appear to hustle full speed ahead. Sure, they appear joyful on the surface, but Martha has shown us what that busyness feels like underneath. In fact, we all know what that frantic rush is like. It may be fun briefly, but it doesn't produce sustainable joy. We must fully believe in the power and promise of our YES. The strength of our decision to put Christ first is the strength that will also fuel our ability to pause when the December marathon starting gun fires. Most of us purposefully start the Christmas race early. We shop ahead, make lists in October, maybe even have gifts wrapped before the Thanksgiving turkey hits the table. Usually, it's all in the name of relaxing more once December rolls around. But how does that truthfully play out for you?

For me, starting early usually just means I add more to the list. Instead of relaxing, I see all that extra time as space to fit in even more ideas and projects. Maybe the better game plan isn't starting earlier, it's starting wiser. Preparing ourselves not just logistically, but spiritually. Getting our hearts in the right place to say a strong yes to what matters and the resulting no to what doesn't. That means intentionally blocking out the frantic so we can keep our focus on the Lord. It's preparing our souls for the challenges of the season before the season starts. Being encouraged by knowing that Jesus tells us this is the right choice. This is our best move. This is how we fill ourselves with what is required for the holiday race ahead. This is the gas pump we need to connect with and fuel our tanks. Only then are we able to peacefully proceed into the chaos the season brings. Only then do we have the discipline to focus daily on Jesus. And isn't that what each of us is looking for? Isn't that what's been missing? It's not the mad rush for presents. It's taking His presence with us and feeling His joy and peace from the beginning to the end of the season...and onward.

Finally, the third aspect I noticed this time in Psalm 23 was the verbs! Our Shepherd isn't passive. He doesn't sit back and hope we figure it out. He's in it with us. He makes, He leads, He restores, He guides, He comforts, He anoints. That's not a distant God. That's a hands-on, heart-close Savior. And us? We get to respond. We get to trust Him, follow Him, rest in Him, and stay with Him. Sure, it's a hard yes at Christmas. But the promise and privilege it offers are so worth it! We can choose to walk through this season personally with the Saviour we are celebrating! That's the invitation of Psalm 23. It's not just poetic or pretty; it's personal and powerful. Jesus doesn't just want to be part of our Christmas season. He wants to be the Shepherd we follow through it.

But what exactly does that mean? Follow. It's an interesting word these days. In biblical times, to follow Jesus meant to surrender to His lordship. It meant forsaking family, home, and even income to share in His life and ministry. He wasn't asking for a casual nod of agreement. He was inviting people into a real relationship. It meant going where He went, listening closely, imitating His heart, and letting His words and ways shape your life from the inside out. It cost something, and it changed everything. Today, when we say we "follow" someone, it usually means we've clicked a little button. There is no personal commitment involved, and we can easily unfollow with another click at any time. Yet this detached observation can influence us tremendously and cause us to reevaluate ourselves or our abilities completely. We've become consumed with highlight reels featuring perfection in any category we choose. As we continue to scroll, we feel the need to do more and to be more. We are indeed changed, but this time from the outside in. The obsessive rush towards perfection outwardly leaves us frantic on the inside. And this is magnified at Christmas!

The call to follow Jesus isn't a social media kind of follow. It's not about watching from afar or admiring Him in theory. It's an everyday decision to walk with Him, learn from Him, and let His presence impact how we live and love, even during or especially during the Christmas season. He wants to actually be with us. The one who provides what we need, even when we don't know what that is. The one who leads us through the chaos, not around it. The one who helps when our joy is depleted and there's still so much to do. Now, that's the kind of Shepherd I need. That's the kind of Shepherd I want to follow, not just at Christmas, but every single day.

So, right now, sipping on my tea, I must say, I'm thinking I might just need to tuck a little shepherd figurine in a prominent spot. Maybe by the sink, on my desk, or riding shotgun in the car, wherever I'll see him often. Maybe even the wallpaper on my phone. Just a tiny, charming reminder that I'm not doing this Christmas season alone. My shepherd is with me. And, I just happen to know where I can find a little wooden shepherd in a nativity set nearby that hopefully won't be missed! Shepherds remind me where real joy comes from, the kind that doesn't hinge on perfect plans, delicious food, or a color-coordinated Christmas. It's the kind of joy that shows up in a manger, steps right into our mess, and fills our hearts right in the middle of it all. The shepherds point me to our good Shepherd, the One who came to show us the way through all the seasons of life, even Christmas. Let's sit with this for a minute. Let's think about who we follow and allow to influence us.

I'll refresh the teapot!

Ponderings 

- Close your eyes and picture following Jesus. Imagine a tough, rocky, steep journey and how He leads you through it rather than walking in an open field of grass. What does it feel like to stay focused on Him and trust Him? Do you focus more on Him or the terrain?

- Think about who you follow on social media. What voices are you letting influence you? Do you need to unfollow anyone to avoid distraction?

- What other distractions pull your focus away from Christ at Christmas?

CHAPTER SIXTEEN

From Chaos to Calm

Let's take a minute to talk about the practice of sitting with Jesus. This time, He clearly tells us through Mary's example that it should come before anything else. Being in His presence is where we start. That's hard for me. Usually, my day starts abruptly with things that need to be done. So, how exactly do we do that? Well, I've learned that it's different for each of us. It's not a formula, and there's no such thing as a perfectly curated quiet time. It can look so many different ways, and we each have to figure that out for ourselves. But here's what it's not. It's not a time to read our wish list as if we were talking to Santa. That's not what Jesus was affirming in Mary. Jesus wants a relationship with you and me. He is not interested in being merely a Santa or a Genie in a bottle. He wants us to get to know Him, to become comfortable being with Him, and to learn to recognize when He is speaking to us. Remember, this speaking is rarely audible, but still very recognizable if you're listening. His goal is to make us more like Him. So this morning time can be a pause, sitting and listening, reading scripture, or following a short devotional. It can even be a time of just intentionally looking out the window and saying good morning to the Lord. It is a time to just be with the Lord, to start with the Lord, to set our focus and release our frantic. It's a time for our daily bread. It's a time to be in His presence, learning to recognize His voice. For those with young children who love to study God's word, this can be frustrating. It is important to recognize that the morning time is focused on inviting Jesus into your day and getting to know Him. Our actual study must take place at a different time. A time when we have longer to dig into God's word. I struggled with this for years and finally realized the benefit of separating these two for that season of my life. Otherwise, my morning time often didn't happen because I didn't feel like I had long enough.

At Christmas, this morning time is like the secret sauce to starting our day on the right foot. If this is totally new for you, even if it's just a quick prayer or a simple thought, acknowledging God's presence and inviting Him into your day makes such a difference! You might say, "Good morning, Lord. I know you're with me today, and I want to follow you." It doesn't have to be anything fancy, just a small, intentional moment to set your heart on Him. The method you use can vary, but the intent must be constant. Also, once you greet the Lord and acknowledge His presence, sit and listen for as long as you can. Remember, Mary was listening to the Lord. It was Martha telling Him what to do. Sure, Martha welcomed Jesus, but only Mary received Him. She did this by staying in His presence. Just sitting in His presence. That little connection can set the daily tone for your whole Christmas season.

Now, I totally understand that mornings can be a whirlwind, and sometimes it feels like there's no time to breathe, let alone spend time in prayer. As you would expect, most mornings I'm scurrying to my hot tea. I've never ever been a morning person, but in this stage of life, it is suiting me quite well, because the definition of early has changed! Yet, for years, I was up early to get my kids to school in the morning, and I know what that looks like. Different seasons of life bring different time demands. If you're someone who usually connects with God later in the day, that's absolutely fine too, and often, as I mentioned, better for study. But it is still so important to start your day with some sort of connection with the Lord. Even as I have mentioned, it is as simple as saying "Good Morning" to the Lord and inviting Him into your day. This allows you to carry Christ with you. And that's an amazing advantage, especially during the Christmas rush. Nothing is going to happen to you at any time that the Lord doesn't already know about. Remember, He already knows everything. There are no surprises for Him. So, isn't it reassuring to already know He is with you as the day comes your way? Spending time with God matters. It's how we invite Him into our lives. It's how He changes our lives. It's how we maintain our joy that we desire for our Christmas season, when everything around us is depleting our supply.

When you establish a bond with Christ in the morning, it is easier to be aware of His presence all day. It's sometimes referred to as *The Practice of the Presence of God*, which is an expression derived from an old and very worthwhile book of the same name, written by Brother Lawrence. It's like bringing Him into everything you do, whether you're doing dishes, writing Christmas cards, or chasing after the kids. God is right there with you, guiding you, strengthening you, and giving you peace in each moment. It can take a little getting used to, so hence the "practice" component is legit!

Living with this constant connection gives you something powerful to lean on throughout your busy day. When things get tough, you're not alone. When challenges come up, you have His strength to carry you. And that's exactly what we need, especially as we try to maintain a sense of joy and peace during the Christmas season. It's just not possible otherwise. So, don't worry if this is new for you. Just start somewhere. Connect with Him in whatever way works for you. But try to do it first thing in your morning. And know that as you do, He's there, ready to walk with you every step of your day.

This awareness of His presence is very helpful because we all know how quickly a peaceful morning can turn chaotic. Especially as your interaction with the outside world begins. Somehow, the Christmas season always takes all normal frustrations up a notch and people's patience down several notches. Tempers are short when people are inconvenienced, and situations can become stressful quickly. All good reasons to know God is walking with us because He brings the calm and order we need. It's His nature.

God has this beautiful way of stepping into chaotic situations throughout the Bible and bringing order. It's like He's always been in the business of creating something beautiful out of messes. Our first image of God is when the world was formless and void. God took what seemed like total chaos and began to bring order to it. The book of Genesis starts with a scene that could feel like the ultimate mess: darkness everywhere, waters swirling, nothing making sense. But then, in just a few simple words, God speaks, and it all starts to come together.

What's remarkably cool here is that God didn't just leave things to chance. No, He actively took chaos and shaped it into something good, with intention, design, and care. And the same God who created and put order in our world is still in the business of bringing order to the chaos in our own lives today. I love that about Him. It is so comforting. He's been making order out of chaos from the very start. And if He can do it with the universe, He can certainly do it in my little orbit and in yours, too, even at Christmas.

We know that Mary chose to spend time with Jesus first, placing Him above everything else. And we also know we can fully trust Jesus as our Shepherd. He cares for us, leads us, and ultimately gave His life to save us. He came to live among us to show us how to live, and His example is our guide. However, we also know how easy it is to become distracted from Him, especially at Christmas. It's so tempting to wander off into unsafe areas, giving in to idols and distractions that pull us away from what truly matters. But when Jesus is with us, even in the midst of the chaos, there can be order, at least, inwardly. He brings peace and clarity to our hearts, no matter what's happening around us.

As you are thinking of things you want to do differently this Christmas, remember how powerful starting your day with God can be. The time spent with the Lord daily, over time, builds an intimate relationship that you can comfortably carry with you and draw from throughout this stressful season. Even better, I think it will enable you to experience Christmas in your heart. Isn't that what we all want? I've been seeking that for years, and I'll be honest, I didn't realize how close joy and fun were to the simple act of spending intentional daily time with Jesus. Somehow, that daily time usually gets sacrificed during the seasonal rush. While we can't continually sit at Jesus' feet, we can start there and continue to feel and enjoy His presence throughout our day. Try committing to this time with Jesus through the Christmas season, even when it gets crazy. See how it changes everything, especially your holiday spirit!

Our God is not a God of chaos. If we let Him, He'll bring order to our mess. He'll bring peace to our panic. He'll bring focus to our frantic. He'll bring order to our overwhelm. It's what Mary chose, and it is the only "yes" that will provide the calm, peace, and joy we are all seeking for the holiday.

Speaking of calm, peace, and joy, well, how about a cup's worth? We are headed from the shepherds in the hills to the Grinch in his chilly hilltop cave! You might want a cup of calm first or at least another warm sip before we move on.

Ponderings 

- How difficult would it be to spend time in the morning with Jesus? What would it look like?

- What areas of your life feel like they are in chaos? How can you invite Christ into that chaos?

- Do you feel like you have an intimate relationship with the Lord? Do you feel His presence during the day? Why or why not?

Part Four

The Good Part

These things I have
spoken to you so that
My joy may be in you,
and that your joy may
be made full.
— John 15:11

When you commit to
a "yes" to Jesus, you
choose joy that lasts.

CHAPTER SEVENTEEN

Advent, Preheat the Oven, Prepare Your Heart

It came without ribbons!

It came without tags!

It came without packages, boxes or bags!

Then the Grinch thought of something he hadn't before!

"Maybe Christmas," he thought, "doesn't come from a store.

Maybe Christmas...perhaps...means a little bit more!"

Seuss[5]

Okay, let me just go ahead and say this up front. If I woke up on Christmas morning and everything was gone, the decorations, the gifts, and especially our annually gifted cream cheese braid, I'm not sure I'd be channeling my inner Who from Whoville. I mean, really. I'd be mad as fire and so disappointed for my kids. And of course, you can be sure the police would be involved with an all-points bulletin out for that cream cheese braid.

---

5   Seuss, Dr. *How the Grinch Stole Christmas!*. Random House, 1957.

Does this mean my heart wasn't properly prepared for Christmas morning? Maybe. Well, probably. But those Whos certainly set a high bar while making an excellent point. They lost everything and still managed to sing in a circle with obvious joy coming from their hearts. Christmas is certainly not about the stuff, and we have talked about that, but a surprise like this on Christmas morning, well, at best, would be hard to handle, and my family wouldn't be singing in any sort of circle.

But this part of their story, while extreme, does remind me of how vital the season of Advent is. It prepares our hearts for Christmas. Not because I'm expecting a grinch to take our presents, but so we can absolutely be ready to celebrate, like the Whos, in our hearts, no matter what's under our tree. Celebrate with true joy that can't be taken from us. Christ's birth, the gift of the first Christmas, is the greatest gift we could ever receive. If we lived in a different culture, one not so tangled up in expectations and performance, it might be easier to focus on and celebrate that gift alone. Here, though, we need a plan, a rhythm to manage the tension between enjoying our cultural traditions while still honoring our Lord's gift.

The church does, however, offer us a helpful source for preparing ourselves for a Christmas focused on Christ. But as more people attend non-denominational churches than ever before, many families aren't familiar with Advent. It seems more people are familiar with Lent, the church season leading into Easter, than with Advent. The word "Advent" comes from the Latin word *adventus*, which means coming or arrival.[6] A very simple explanation of this church season is that it begins four Sundays before December 25th and is a time of spiritual preparation and waiting. The season is observed in many Christian traditions that follow a liturgical calendar. Traditionally, it's a time to slow down, reflect, and make room, not just on our calendars, but in our hearts for the true gift of Christmas, Jesus Himself. It reminds us that just like the world waited for the Messiah long ago, we're still expectantly waiting today for Him to renew us and one day return.

If your holiday tradition includes Advent, you might be thinking that this is what I've been talking about when I've suggested starting wiser and preparing spiritually for Christmas. But it's not. Stay with me here. Because Christmas now starts before our Thanksgiving turkey is even cooked, if we're not careful, we'll race or scroll to grab the early sales and never look back. Our culture jumps straight from pumpkins to poinsettias, and it's very easy to jump right along with it. It's fun. It's what we wait all year for, right? Who doesn't like a season of indulgence? There is absolutely a lot to celebrate in December, and I'm all for the fun! December is an incredible month. But we can't let the parties and the plans drown out the purpose. That's when we find ourselves slipping back into the frantic, chasing the perfect, and missing the ever-elusive heartfelt Christmas we desire. It's just so easy to get caught up in all the stuff. In fact, it's so easy that despite our best intentions, it happens year after year.

---

6   "Advent." *Merriam-Webster.com Dictionary*, Merriam-Webster, https://www.merriam-webster.com/dictionary/Advent. Accessed 16 Aug. 2025.

That's why it helps so much to come into Advent already anchored. If we begin preparing spiritually before the season ramps up (sitting with Jesus) and we've already centered our hearts on Jesus (practicing His presence), then it's a whole lot easier to stay focused as the Christmas chaos begins. A focused heart going into Advent is what helps keep us attentive through it. It's what makes it special and not just something we "should" do. Otherwise, the season sweeps us up, and before we know it, we're racing to December 25th with unburnt Advent candle wicks, like mine, and empty hearts. If we're not in the habit of sitting at Jesus' feet daily, it's a hard time to start once the season is coming at us. We need to be more focused on and recommitted to our relationship with the Lord in advance. As we talked about earlier, we need to be game-ready. That starts when we follow our Shepherd closely. Jesus' affirmation of Mary's yes influences our yes. Our yes influences our family's yes. What better gift could we give them?

Speaking of Mary, let's take another look at Jesus' visit that day. Both sisters welcomed Jesus into their home. The scripture gives us the impression that Martha welcomed Him and pretty quickly went back to keep working. Serving Him, so that everything was nice for her guest to enjoy. Mary, on the other hand, not only welcomed Him, but also received Him. She did this by staying with Him, sitting at His feet, and listening to what He had to say. Obviously, there's a difference here. Stop and think about it. Jesus is showing me that this is exactly what I do at Christmas. Sure, I welcome Christmas! I welcome it with open arms and dive in immediately with all the preparations. In my mind, I'm serving my family to provide them with a magical, meaningful holiday. The problem is, I never stop to receive Christmas like Mary received Jesus. I never stop and sit with Jesus and receive what He so wants to give me personally. The happy energy that welcomed Christ at the beginning of the season is replaced with a tired, frustrated, empty heart, wondering where Jesus is in all this. Thankfully, the season of Advent gives us the structure to stop and receive Jesus, but also prepare to celebrate Him well in our hearts.

So, while the Grinch's heart grew three sizes in one dramatic moment, we get a whole season to let ours soften and stretch. Advent gives us time and space to prepare, not our homes, but our hearts. To prepare to celebrate the greatest gift the world has ever been given. Advent prepares us to inwardly and outwardly welcome Christmas morning because it brings our long-awaited Redeemer! Many churches provide Advent curriculums to facilitate a spiritual rhythm for the four weeks. I'm sure you've also seen Advent devotional books. Often, families have an Advent wreath on a table that they put candles on, lighting an additional one each week leading up to Christmas.

Is celebrating Advent part of your church or family tradition? I've certainly had more success in some years than others. Do you manage to light all your candles? We've talked about having a game plan to be ready spiritually when December gets here. This enables us to feel prepared to handle the minefields that lie ahead during the Christmas Season. And in fact, I should use these words correctly, especially now that we are talking specifically about Advent. The Christmas season, from the Church's standpoint, doesn't start till Christmas Day. It is after Advent and lasts for twelve days, just like the song. Culturally, Christmas begins when you want it to! Because of this difference in timing, over the years, the Advent season has become very counter-cultural. As we've noted, most of us are in full Christmas mode as soon as the Thanksgiving dishes are done! We are singing the songs, having the parties, watching the movies, and enjoying all the cultural aspects of the season. Our culture can't get enough of the season that gives us permission to buy, buy, buy, and indulge with more, more, more. In fact, I remember when Christmas ads didn't start till Thanksgiving weekend. Imagine! But now there is a constant media blitz starting in October aimed directly at us, telling us what we must have or must do for the perfect Christmas. Of course, we know now that there is no such thing as a perfect Christmas. Even the night Jesus was born was messy, but it was holy, and the eternal gift was given. As we begin to shift our perspective to see Christmas more as a gift we receive, not something we have to produce, we make space in our hearts to personally celebrate. And like so many things in our walk with Jesus, it's a choice. A better choice. One that leads to lasting joy. Because once we choose to center our hearts on Christ, that joy can't be taken from us. In the end, we get to decide: Will this be a Christmas that draws us closer to Him or one that leaves us worn out and empty?

Walking with Christ and navigating our family through Advent can be so much fun and is quite a privilege. It's also a way to reinforce our own time with the Lord and encourage our family to do the same. Does your family have a nativity set that you place somewhere special each year? When our kids were young, our set took center stage and came alive as we marked each passing day of Advent. Every night we would celebrate and add another piece, slowly constructing the scene of Jesus' birth. We would start with our empty stable placed in its spot. That first night, we would prepare the stable by scattering hay around for the animals that would arrive next. As we did this, we discussed how we, too, were preparing to receive Jesus in our hearts. (Throughout the rest of December, the kids were given additional hay to add when they were helpful around the house.)

The second night, we would add the cows. There are so many great young children's books about the animals at Jesus' birth, and we would read one or two that night. One night would be shepherds, again reading in the Bible and/or a children's book about their presence that holy night. A fun evening was sheep night as those plump pieces were added to our growing scene. Depending on the age of your children, you can do Mary and Joseph together or separate them into two nights, discussing their stories leading up to this special night. Or you can place them on the other side of the house and let them slowly progress towards the nativity each day, even hiding them along the way. You may have a donkey to celebrate, too! Again, it is amazing the books you can find to celebrate all these participants at Jesus' birth. There are even fun songs that you can sing together.

BUT, our scene is not complete! What's missing? Well, of course, the Wise Men, their camels, and Jesus. This is where we depart from the traditional version of the nativity. Traditionally, in our family, the youngest child would hide baby Jesus and place him in the manger on Christmas morning. Obviously, there were years that we didn't FIND baby Jesus until much later. Then, what about those wise men? The Bible tells us that the wise men were nowhere near Bethlehem when Jesus was born. They came a good two years later, following the star to find the baby. So, in our house, the wise men with their gifts and camels are on the other side of the room! Again, there are great children's books and, more importantly, a children's Bible to read about their story.

These bedtimes are such great memories for all of us. Even now, decades later, as I set up our nativity, I am reminded of those times together. It is a fun tradition that can last for generations. This year, I'll be dusting all my books off to celebrate the scene of God's magical gift with my very young grandchildren. Davy, our youngest, will be 15 months, so no telling where or when baby Jesus will be found! Maybe He'll be near the missing shepherd ... just saying.

There is room in Advent for many variations. Is your family musical? There are so many great options for you to try with songs and instruments, or having people over for an old-fashioned sing-along. What about the readers out there? You can go crazy over all the children's and young adult books for Christmas that teach and focus on Jesus.

What about a special tree with meaningful religious decorations depicting Jesus' birth? This is called a Chrismon tree, a special type of Christmas tree decorated only with Christian symbols called Chrismons, which is short for "Christ monograms." These symbols represent aspects of Jesus' life, ministry, and identity. Items like crosses, doves, fish, stars, crowns, and Greek letters like Alpha and Omega.

Artists out there. Draw the story and create a family Advent book! Make a list of all the things that changed for us when Jesus was born. There are so many ways to bring Christ into your Advent and genuinely observe a season of waiting and watching for the newborn king, not just reevaluating your Christmas list. Planning a way to engage your children during Advent is so important. They won't have anyone else doing it for them except maybe at church. Otherwise, they will surely just be consumed by a worldly holiday and miss so much.

What about yourself? This can be a lonely effort, unless you seek fellowship with your Christian friends. As friends, we can hold each other accountable, but more importantly, we can encourage each other throughout this fast-paced, but seemingly long season. Calling, texting, visiting, or even dropping off silly gifts can help us all remember we are not alone in this. By trading perfection for peace and chaos for calm every step of the way, we can maintain our Mary stance. Reminding each other to start with Jesus every day when the world is publicizing and screaming for our inner Martha everywhere. If we can hold firm with our focus, it is much more likely that we will arrive at Christmas filled with the joy we have longed for. And if we have done it with our friends, it will mean all the more.

So, Advent can be the framework or key to keeping the season for your whole family as it was meant to be. A celebration of God's gift to us all. Sending His Son to save the world. A gift that needs to be welcomed and also received! Who would ever imagine that this incredible message could get overshadowed, but we live in a world full of distracted people. I'm recommitting to Advent this year, and I am excited about how it will serve as a good marker for me on how my priorities for the season are playing out. Because by committing myself to stay in a daily relationship with the Lord, I can do a much better job of sharing His joy and peace with those around me. Helping them remember and also celebrate, honor, and better understand the priceless eternal gift that is the reason for the season, Jesus. Join me?

Advent time with your family can be so cozy, just like those quiet, early mornings with the Lord. And there's something just as comforting about sitting with a friend who's walking beside you through the crazy Christmas season. It kind of makes me want to clink mugs. Cheers, friend!

Ponderings 

- Do you welcome **and receive** Christ at Christmas? What does that look like?

- We've talked about idols already, but can you think of anything else that you allow to overshadow the miracle of the first Christmas?

- What would honoring Advent look like for your family?

- Do you have a friend that you could partner with to encourage and pray for each other through the season?

CHAPTER EIGHTEEN

Season Opener, A Tradition Unlike Any Other

I've been looking forward to telling you about our family's Season Opener. Please know it is not my intention here to add anything that would create more Christmas chaos for you. Rather, I hope it will inspire you to look at your own traditions and figure out how or if they could work better for your family or even evolve with your family. We should not be slaves to our traditions. They should work for us. We've talked earlier about how some traditions serve their purpose and come to an end. It's not a bad thing. They then become cherished memories instead of forced rituals.

This particular tradition is one that has evolved so beautifully through the years. It worked well when our children were young, when they were tweens, and it even continues to delight now with grandchildren on board. It didn't start with the intention of grounding our Christmas with Christ, but it has evolved (as I have evolved) into a wonderful, fun way to begin the season focused on what it's all about. If we could only have one family Christmas tradition, I'm pretty confident this would be chosen unanimously.

It's a tradition with roots that go back to my in-laws. Each year, when they decorated their tree, they had a fun dinner at which Bob and his sisters received new ornaments that reflected highlights from their past year. Other gifts included festive Christmas ceramics and all sorts of holiday things as they got older and had their own homes. It was a fun, simple evening and a tradition I definitely wanted to continue. We started it the same way, with our kids getting new ornaments each year when we decorated the tree. We would have a fun dinner and put a Christmas movie on in the background. As time passed, they each started their own Christmas collection that was added to each year. For Ashley, it was Babushka dolls, for Bo it was Nutcrackers, and Mac collected snow globes and later, snow village pieces. Then pajamas were added and books, toys, and anything Christmas, so each year it just got bigger. Do you have trouble leaving well enough alone? Trust me, I do, and I'm not encouraging it. But stay with me. The evolution of this tradition (and me) hadn't started yet.

Then, when our son Bo brought his girlfriend (now wife), Mary Rachel, for the first time, she brilliantly named it the Season Opener, and the name stuck. We re-established that it was to be a fun, casual night with favorite foods and lots of surprises. And through the years, it was indeed that. As the kids all became adults, we modified it a bit, adding some games and more functional seasonal gifts for their homes. It was always early in December or even the weekend after Thanksgiving if they were all here. Basically, we opened the season together and toasted the month to come. With time, though, it became more like a second Christmas as I bought more and more gifts, and the table became much more of a thing! The meal got away from "simple" as I eagerly swayed (really jumped) into a Martha tilt. The tradition itself remained wonderful, but I got carried away with always trying to make it better. Not one person requested I take it up this notch, but like Clark with his Christmas lights, I was sure it was adding to their holiday enjoyment. So there were many years that I was really hosting two Christmases, each one quite the production. That exhaustion is a large factor behind this book. I was totally serving the tradition and making it an idol. The tradition itself was good, but this Martha desperately needed to make a Mary tilt, for everybody's sake.

Of course, God knew all this, and He began whispering, *"Ann, Ann (Martha, Martha), you are worried and upset about many things"*. It took some time, but eventually I listened as my frustration grew into desperation. All the seasonal distractions we've talked about just crashed in on me, and I knew I was getting Christmas all wrong. I'm so thankful I finally listened and continue to listen to His caring, loving voice, reminding me to always start at His feet. This is also when God began to put this book on my heart. I can assure you, my answer was "You've got the wrong girl!" Christmas was just all too much, and I was mixed up on my priorities. I even found myself glad a couple of years ago when the season was over, and once again disappointed that it was not a spiritual experience for me. Looking back, I can see it so clearly, I was totally striving for perfection in every part of the season. The meals, the gifts, the table, absolutely everything. And as we all know by now, that kind of striving doesn't leave much room for Jesus. All that effort left me exhausted and empty. While there seemed to be plenty of joy out there in the world, there was absolutely no joy in me. But again, the problem was not with this tradition. It was with me.

I knew I was going overboard, and deep down, I eventually realized that no one was asking me to do it all except, well, me. The truth is, the fun was already there. It was in all of us just being together within the framework of a simple tradition. Sure, the gifts were a hit, they always are, but I didn't need to get so many, or present them so dramatically, or labor over such a fancy dinner. Once again, I needed to listen to my favorite Mary Poppins line, "Enough is as good as a feast." But much more than that, Jesus was showing me the difference between welcoming Him only and receiving Him fully.

Now that I've entered the grandparent era, something else in me has shifted, nudging me toward a new way of seeing the season. A simpler way, like when my own kids were little, and wonder didn't come from excess, but from presence. Without taking away a single necessary sparkle from our Season Opener (because you know I still love the fun!), my heart is leaning more and more toward Jesus. I'm remembering how deeply He loves us, and that all the joy flows from Him, not from the beauty of my celebration. And honestly? It feels refreshing. It feels right. It's like the beginning of a gentle, but fully committed tilt back toward Mary.

To help you understand a little better, I'll tell you about last year's Opener. Instead of starting in the splash of the dining room, we all started the evening in an interior hallway, with all the lights off. The space was pitch black since there were no windows. All the grandchildren were sitting on the floor with me, and one lucky grown-up was holding our very young Davy. I had a flashlight (off at the moment), and we talked about the world living in darkness and what darkness felt like. At five, three, two, and four months, their answers were what you would expect. "Can't see." " Scary." "Don't know where anyone is". Then I turned on the flashlight, and we all saw what a difference one light made. It made us feel safer, and we could see our way to walk. I told them the presence of light represented Jesus coming into the world. He broke up the darkness that everyone had felt and showed us how to live. We also remarked that even though He helps us see, we still can't see Him. We mentioned how He talks to us through our hearts, not our ears, to teach and lead us. This was the second year we had started in the dark hallway, and we will probably do the same thing for another year or two. The repetition is good, and soon the older ones will be showing the younger ones themselves. It sets the tone and leads into wonderful continuing conversations for the current season and in future years. And do know, for us, this took all of about 5 minutes! It's easy to fit in, even with little ones. Sure, they already know some Bible stories and even some simple verses, but painting some broad strokes to put it all together is helpful for them and will help them connect the dots to know Jesus better. This alone would be a nice activity to do with young children, followed by a treat of some sort. For our Opener, though, we went straight to the dining room (now the North Pole) for a festive meal! The North Pole was where their Christmas supplies were waiting for them. As the doors opened, snowflakes were dropping from the ceiling (thank you, Ashley), and there were presents and fun treats on the table. Once everyone had arrived at the Pole, we had a fabulous Chick-fil-A meal that was delivered for a no-stress dinner, which everyone loved.

After dinner, everyone had a ribbon streamer at their place, each one winding its way to their special presents. Among the books they received were Christ-centered stories to keep hearts focused on the reason we celebrate. It was fun and simple. The children each opened ornaments, puzzles, books, and little games selected especially for them. The grownups received wrapping supplies and seasonal items to use around their homes. Some of their childhood collections are still growing, which just adds to the fun.

It's such a special event; everyone is just as excited about what others are receiving as they are about their own gifts. And the best part? Not only does each person leave with something new to enjoy, but this is also a pause and a beginning reflection on the season. At the end of the meal and presents, we declare the season open and toast to the weeks ahead. We ended the night in our PJs playing nativity charades.

So that is what our Season Opener looked like this past year, as it continues to evolve. Instead of being seen as a second Christmas, now it is the only time we are all together during the season. Because of this, it has become a whole weekend, since so many are traveling to be here. It is a tradition that no one wants to discontinue, and at this time in our lives, it is particularly fun because it brings us all together.

And that's another reason I thought this was worth mentioning. It is a fun way to have everyone together early in the season, especially when it's not possible to all be together for Christmas itself. As families grow and people move, it gets harder to all be together on Christmas Day. As

I mentioned, the opener has become the only time we are all together for Christmas and lasts a weekend. It's not a Martha tilt, but just an adjustment to the tradition that suits our family stage now. The Martha tilt is avoided because I've learned how simpler is better and actually adds space for joy. We have started having reindeer games during the day. Winners collect fluffy snowballs to throw at Santa at the conclusion of the games. We also started fireside chats at bedtime with the new weekend format. Of course, it was way too warm for a fire this past year, but we still gathered around the hearth anyway. It was honestly a very dear time. We talked some more about Jesus' birth and read books. We also played nativity charades, and that was a big hit. The kids asked questions, and we just had fun being together in a simple setting as opposed to the fun chaos of the actual party. I can not recommend this enough if it would work in your family's situation and if you can fight the urge to overdo it. Simple is the key.

There are so many variations you could do on this theme! It just depends on the age of your family and what you can manage without making a Martha tilt. One thing is for sure, though. This is a great way to start the season with Jesus. Whether it's in a dark hallway or acting out the nativity, telling each other the story in turns, or even coloring, the possibilities are endless. Young adult children would also benefit from learning more about Jesus' birth, especially aspects that are not well-known. Also, it's never too early to learn about what we have been discussing, deliberately spending time with Jesus in the midst of the rush. Dare I say it one more time? There are so many great Advent books and devotionals available now to help you start the season strong.

Obviously, this scale of an event or even the event itself is certainly not a necessary addition to the season. Once you understand Who your joy comes from and the only way it can be sustained, evaluate everything you do during the holidays in that light. For us, this tradition has been worth adjusting over the years and has grown with our family. Its significance has deepened as I've grown, learning to seek a more meaningful Christmas. A simple evening decorating the tree with some special ornaments is a wonderful way to start the season, and what we did for years. Nativity ornaments and books are great ways to focus on Jesus from the beginning. I have found it very helpful, especially now with online shopping, to buy all of the next year's opener gifts during after-Christmas sales. They are at least half price, and I just store them away and pull them out when it's time. It really makes it so easy the next year and doesn't add anything to your Christmas shopping list.

Remember, don't add this to your current traditions if it is too much. This would definitely be a Martha tilt and exhaust you just as the season is getting started. Keep it in mind for another season of life. It truthfully is a great grandparent suggestion if your family is scattered, and it would be easier to all be together in early December or right after Thanksgiving. I share this idea because it can be a great way to begin the season on the right track. The theme can start the season with the right focus, on Jesus. As I said, it is pretty easy to pull off, especially if you can buy what you are giving everyone a year in advance. Then all you have to do is the meal...and for us, nowadays, that always comes in the form of delivery or takeout!

Have you ever heard the expression that begins, "The best laid plans..."? Well, the Lord taught me a lesson this past year that I didn't see coming, and it certainly wasn't included in my best-laid plans. I'd love to spare you from learning it the hard way. So sit back, and lean in a little closer, because what I learned gave me a fresh perspective on the season. I think it might just speak to your heart, too.

We don't want to rush this. Refill your mug and let's continue when you're ready.

Ponderings 

- How do you find ways to bring Jesus into the Christmas celebration with adults and with children?

- Do your traditions work for you, or do you work for them?

- Do you feel a need to reevaluate your family's Christmas traditions?

CHAPTER NINETEEN

Nana's Down

I'm not quite sure how long we had been in the emergency room. I was in so much pain, I wasn't even opening my eyes to embrace any more of the situation than necessary. It had all happened so fast, and in that split second, so much shifted. Tripper, my 5-year-old grandson, and I were challenging Bob in a basketball game. T and I were both on fire, and I had just sunk my third shot in a row! I was feeling cocky and confident as I backpedaled into position for us to continue. We had this game in the bag. Before I knew it, even though in my mind it happened in slow motion, I was on the ground, consumed by pain, and my left hand was confused about where it was supposed to be. Nana (yep, that's me) was down, and it didn't look good.

Let's pause here because there are some things you need to know. First, I am not particularly athletic. I was ecstatic that I had made those three baskets. Second, in my family, I am surrounded by athletes. So, I was even more ecstatic that I had made three baskets back-to-back! Third, it was December 17th. Take this last one in for a moment and move on when you understand this game-changing point...

Originally, I had planned for this book to come out a year ago. But then I had decided to wait and spend one more Christmas talking to moms and asking if they struggled at

Christmas, and if so, what they struggled with. I just wanted to make sure my book would be helpful. I knew God wanted me to write this book, and I knew I wanted to read this book! Sort of a strange combination for an author, but the Lord was asking me to make my mess my message. As is His nature, He has been very faithful throughout this process. He is teaching me and writing this message on my heart as I put it on paper for your heart also.

I hope you've seen in my honesty that I am indeed a fellow struggler with all the distractions Christmas brings. My desire for holiday magic and perfection with all aspects of our celebration has left me exhausted for years. I finally realized that something had to change. I wanted more for myself than just giving others a magical experience. I wanted to feel again the spiritual significance of Jesus' birth personally. I wanted to arrive at Christmas Eve with a new, refreshed appreciation for what God had done not only for mankind, but for me. Yet, the frustrating truth is, the joy, the spirit of thankfulness, and awe just got lost. Usually, somewhere around the time that I also realized my time with the Lord had unfortunately been pushed aside. That time had been reallocated to the pull of the post-it notes and disappeared. I was making the annual Martha tilt.

As I was learning more about the struggles women face at Christmas, I decided to try doing things a little differently myself, slowing down and being more intentional about my time and priorities, especially how I started each day. I also wanted to see what my family's reaction would be to things not being as polished as usual. The Lord must have had some doubts about my "slowdown" commitment. Maybe because it had never worked before? Apparently, He felt I needed a little encouragement to take it easy. Otherwise, why would I have shattered my wrist on December 17th? I've never had a broken bone in my life. Whatever the reason, my Christmas plans shifted that afternoon, and so did my family's. And while it was an accident, it was also no accident as the Lord certainly wasn't surprised. His ways are not our ways, but they are always good.

It's not in my personality to surrender easily. All the women in my family before me and after me, well, we are a strong-willed group. With current ages from 3 to 91, we are a force for our fellas to deal with. But when the Lord says sit, and you haven't been listening, well, sometimes you fall. And just like that, I had time to sit with God during December. This was definitely not a Mary tilt but a downright shove! And Jesus was teaching me its value, especially at Christmas.

One thing that has always baffled me is why I or anyone would find it a struggle to spend time sitting with God. Stop and think about it. God! The creator and sustainer of everything that exists. He gives us access to Himself and even desires that we pursue Him. He manages every aspect of our world, but always has time for us. He speaks a word and things come into being, and yet He still wants to speak to you and me! Such infinite power combined with such infinite love, yet always waiting patiently for us to seek Him. Why aren't we waking up each morning ecstatically seeking Him and eager to share our new day with Him? We should be joyfully delighted to be in His presence! Just like Mary sitting at Jesus' feet. Where else would she possibly be? What in the world could keep us from that? The crazy, unfortunate answer that we all know and certainly Martha knew is summed up in one word: distractions.

We've talked at length about what distractions are. But we haven't talked about the fact that they, by themselves, are powerless. We give them their power. We chase them. We see them and invite them in. But when we do that, it means we are squeezing something else out. You and I both know what that is. We replace our time with Jesus with something else. Something that has attracted our attention and become oh so important that we have to do it or we have to have it, and we can think of nothing else. Something that we feel will bring us quick satisfaction. Perhaps like a picture-perfect Christmas. In other words, an idol.

We forego what we desperately need in order to accomplish what we desperately want, a perfect Christmas for our loved ones. In other words, we forego the best part. The One who loves us most of all, the One who patiently waits and holds all the answers we seek, is pushed aside. Such craziness! The intimacy we get in following Jesus is worth much more than any perceived quick satisfaction from anyone or anything else. It's such an obviously bad decision, but so easily done. Remember, it's just a tilt, not even a pivot.

Now, back to Nana's wrist. Surgery was performed, hardware installed, and home I went. Once home, I sat and slept and sat. December, meanwhile, was ticking by quietly in the background. Ashley and Bob stuffed and stamped the Christmas cards to get them out on time, and Ashley especially tried hard to keep us on track. As the initial fog of anesthesia and chaos began to lift, I realized just how quickly December was slipping away without any assistance from me. Thankfully, my family seemed aware of the ticking clock, and they all jumped in to "save" Christmas. And what exactly does that even mean, "saving Christmas"? The Grinch has made it clear: Christmas comes whether we have all the decorations and perfectly manicured traditions or not. Still, the meals and the little rituals matter. They are what help us mark the season.

Eventually, just like every other year, Christmas came and went, ready or not. Afterwards, I asked everyone how my injury had affected their holiday. Normally, I don't let them do much because Mary Rachel and Sydney are juggling little ones, Ashley's deep in the trenches of Christmas ministry life, and Bo and Mac are each busy with work now. All these factors motivate my mom brain to provide a stress-free, magical setting for them to enjoy. Why do we do this? Is it just me? I feel compelled to offer a respite from their hectic lives. But this year God had a different plan. So I wondered. Did they feel less joy? More pressure? Did carrying more responsibility take away from the season? Sydney and Mac weren't with us this year, so they weren't as affected, although Sydney did provide top-notch online shopping support! Mary Rachel immediately started deciding what really needed to happen and what could gracefully "slide" given the circumstances. She and Ashley teamed up on the menus and did all of the food prep. Ashley, bless her, had the extra challenge of managing both her mom's Christmas traditions and her dad's expectations, which, let's just say, leaned heavily toward wanting everything perfect for me. Honestly, he may have been a tad over-helpful at times. So Bo graciously took on the added role of managing Dad! But you know what? They all said they actually enjoyed coming together. The table was decorated with our grandson Tripper's creative flair, and there were even a few dance breaks in the kitchen. It was different, but it was fun. Once again, God showed me that He alone is their respite and their source of joy. My role is to live my faith authentically, embracing joy and peace, and guiding them toward its true source. This is true no matter what age our children are. It was a powerful and necessary reminder of an obvious but often forgotten truth.

And what else did I learn? Well, apparently, Christmas can happen without me orchestrating every detail. Turns out the "magic" comes from the laughter, the teamwork, and the being together. It's not from the perfectly folded napkins or carefully shaped butter. I felt so loved and cared for. They handled it all so well, even while managing their own work and family responsibilities. I did notice the stress in their eyes at times, though, and couldn't help but wonder if that's what they always see in mine?

But here's the part I'll never forget: I experienced what it was like to receive Christmas. I felt present in a way I hadn't in years. I had time to read with the kids, chat with the grown-ups, and just be. Time to sit at Jesus' feet. Time to connect with those who are dear to me. Time to reflect and attempt to count my blessings. I remember sitting there, completely overwhelmed by love. Love for my family and love for Jesus. It was a lot to process. And no, that's not a complaint. Not even close. By slowing down and also by not taking on any added distractions, I was able to experience the one thing, the best part. I was able to abide with Jesus (and Advil). It can be done even without a medical reason. But then it involves a choice.

A committed choice and a bold choice. It is the best choice, and next year I plan to make it for myself. Christmas still happened without me at the wheel. Christmas still happened without me "creating it". Sure, I had help (and I learned to accept it) getting things done, but there was no striving for any standard other than just having fun. With that simplicity, I was able to be present in the moment as well as abide in God's presence the whole time. Those two are big and I wish them for you, minus the broken bones of course.

Speaking of wishing, I also wish for you one more fresh cup of tea! We are almost done, but we need to go back and pull it all together.

Ponderings 

- Have you ever been forced to be still by an event or injury? What did you learn?

- Do you take our unlimited access to God for granted? Would viewing it as the privilege it is change your commitment to spending time with the Lord?

CHAPTER TWENTY

Mary and Bright

It's been both a blessing and somewhat of a surprise to share my journey with you. A blessing, because after talking with so many women, I've come to realize I'm not crazy. Turns out, a lot of us struggle with Christmas. My hope is that by sharing my own frustrations, I have encouraged you in yours. Just knowing we're not alone in all this unquestionably makes a difference. The surprise part? Well, writing a book has never been on my bucket list or any list, for that matter. I barely survived freshman English, and my success story there, well, that's a whole different tale for another time. These pages before you honestly have been written by the Lord on my heart, along with the desire to share them with you. It is, as they say, my mess becoming my message. We were never meant to walk alone, especially in our faith. We need each other, shoulder to shoulder, tea in hand, cheering each other on in our journey. So many of us find ourselves worn out year after year chasing the image of a perfectly manicured Christmas for our families. By the time October rolls around, the TV ads and social media posts are already in full swing. Telling us, yet again, what Christmas should look like from top to bottom. And somehow, each year we jump right back in with new optimism that this will be the year we will manage the balance between the peace we so desire and the perfection we feel is so required.

Yet time and again, we end up weary and exhausted, quietly disappointed and longing for something more. It just seems so simple. All we want is a Christmas celebration that gives us room to celebrate in our hearts, just like we celebrate under our tree. Right? And with what the Lord continues to teach me, I know that when I jump back in this year, I'm going in better equipped than ever before. I want to walk into Christmas with a heart that's more prepared than my Christmas table. I want to go into the season wiser. I want to feel Jesus' presence personally and for my family to know the same. Not just through what I do for them, but through the joy that comes from being with Him. Are you with me?

Hopefully, the Christmas lens on Mary and Martha has been helpful. It's challenged me in the best of ways, and I hope it's stirred something in you, too. Sitting with Jesus first thing every morning is just the most successful pattern I have seen in others and certainly what Jesus models for us in scripture. As we mentioned, the time spent doesn't have to be long, but it does need to be intentional. Our discipline to maintain this habit can only last if it is matched by an equally high commitment, though. Instead of doing what we want or what appeals to us in the moment, in this case, we need to stay focused on how we want to feel on Christmas Day. For that discipline, there's just no substitute for time in His presence. When we start with Him, we carry His peace into our day. He calms our chaos and sharpens our focus. And we need that, especially with all the noise, distractions, and shiny idols that pull at us this time of year. By choosing this Mary tilt, we have the strength to focus on what is truly important each day and prepare our celebration from a place of joy. Not desperately seeking approval from or trying to impress others, but responding to God's love with sincerely joyful and thankful hearts for what He has done. Because that's what it's all about. God's gift to the world that night, some 2000 years ago, was and will always be Christmas.

The movie *Christmas Vacation* has always been a family favorite. In fact, my son Bo can pretty much recite the movie line by line, any time, anywhere. I'm referring to the movie again because it offers yet another faith nugget. In one particular scene, Cousin Eddie tries to look on the bright side of the very disappointing and unexpected change in the company Christmas gift his brother, Clark, received that year. Instead of the usual bonus, each employee received a membership in a jelly of the month club. So, in an attempt to lift everyone's spirits as this disappointing gift is opened, he describes it as the "gift that keeps on giving". Well, cousin Eddie was spot on with the jelly club, but his answer can also speak to something much deeper. By sending His only Son into the world to save us and teach us, God gave us the ultimate gift that keeps on giving. God created Christmas. That's been done. We don't have to create it, we receive it and celebrate it!.

Do you feel ready to say a strong yes? Do you know what you are saying "yes" to? You are saying yes to the same choice Mary made, the decision to put spending time with Jesus before anything else. You're saying yes to Jesus being the center of your Christmas. You are saying yes to a joy that can not be taken from you. Are you ready to choose unlimited refills for your cup of joy? Are you ready to celebrate Christmas in your heart as well as under your tree? Are you ready for less distraction and more devotion? Our "yes" will help all the necessary "nos" fall in place. And while this little pep talk sounds happy and motivating, we need to stop and remember how we got here, why we started, and also realize how we are going to need each other.

We started with our very first kettle of tea, talking about how unseen we often feel during the Christmas season. While the cheery Christmas songs play on repeat and the lights twinkle from every corner, we can feel exhausted, overwhelmed, and anything but joyful. All we hear is culture yelling for us to do more, be more, and buy more! Like the duck gliding calmly across the water, underneath, we're paddling like crazy, trying to hold everything together. It's discouraging, especially when this frantic rhythm plays on for days and days and days. Like Martha in her kitchen, we find ourselves asking, "Lord, don't You care?"

Then, we turned to the distractions that pull our focus from Christ and create the isolation and frustration that Martha felt. And wow, the season is full of them. They're shiny, tempting, and basically good things. But when they call to us from every corner, promising joy, fulfillment, and even identity, well then, they quietly become idols. They convince us that they offer everything we need, but they never quite deliver. For Martha, her distraction was serving. For us, it can be anything we become obsessed with during the holiday: our homes, our social calendars, our clothes, our gifts to others, or anything else. Somehow, our culture has convinced us that Christmas gives us permission to overindulge in any way we choose. Yet, our culture doesn't tell us what constant striving, emptiness, and loneliness this can lead to.

After that, we left Martha and focused on Mary. What made her choose differently from her sister? We looked at the choice Mary made and how powerful that choice was then and still is today. This ancient choice still matters today, especially during the Christmas season. But it can feel like a nearly impossible choice to make. Mary chose Jesus first, before anything that needed to be done. And while that sounds simple in theory, it was bold. She chose presence over performance. She chose worship over service. Today, we face that same dilemma. Where does Jesus come in our daily schedule? Mary said first. He comes first. That should be our answer also. When we begin our day at His feet, we're filled with the strength and peace we need to live the way He's calling us to. But it's not easy. It takes intention. It takes a strong yes. A yes to acknowledging Christ's presence and to desiring to walk with Him through whatever your day brings. The kind of yes that anchors us and sets our feet on a path behind our Good Shepherd. A Shepherd we can trust. A Shepherd who knows exactly where we need to go. And a Shepherd who lovingly leads us there, one step at a time.

Sure, we can read this and feel all fired up, but let me remind you what I am learning. The isolation we felt when we first met will continue if we don't actively seek fellowship and support. These changes will be much easier to make if you have a friend or friends determined to do this with you. Encouraging each other definitely helps when the season gets crazy and the noise of distractions is coming at you constantly. Knowing we are all in this together is vital. Another helpful tool might be writing yourself or a friend some notes to open during the four weeks of Advent. These could be anything from scripture to fun coupons, anything that would help you remember and celebrate what you have said yes to.

Finally, and this is so important, celebrate Christmas in a way that feels like you. Not the way Instagram or our culture insists, but the way that God uniquely created you to enjoy. He's given you gifts and talents that bring you joy. Those are meant to be used! So go ahead. If you love baking, bake your heart out. If decorating makes you light up, deck the halls. If you're all about a beautifully set table, have fun setting it well. But here's the key: don't fall into the trap of thinking you have to do all these things and do them perfectly. That's when the joy slips away, the Post-it notes collect, and Jesus starts to get squeezed out. That's when Christmas becomes a performance instead of a celebration. For me, that's when the season itself becomes an idol.

There's so much to celebrate at Christmas! Just imagine the difference it would make if each of us simply worshipped our Savior by celebrating Him with the gifts He's already given us. Creating a celebration from our heart and our passions. Using our creativity, our love, and our energy, not to impress anyone, but to honor Him. After all, it is His birthday, right?

I can't help but think that this would absolutely delight His heart, and fill ours, too. So come on. Let's stop striving to meet the culture's impossible standard of perfection at Christmas. We never will. And we know that trying will only leave us exhausted and empty. But when we use our gifts from Him, with Him, and for Him, we'll find ourselves filled with the kind of joy that can't be manufactured. It can only be received. The kind of joy that can not be taken away because we are connected to its source.

As little girls, for most of us, it was easy to live in a state of joy. We were blessed with a place to live and parents who loved us. Being ourselves was enough. The days were carefree, and we fell into our beds at night exhausted. I know that isn't everyone's story, and my heart aches for those who didn't have that kind of childhood. But for me, it was a happy time, and one of my favorite memories was how much I loved to twirl. Did you twirl? Do you remember the feeling of being giddy with joy? I felt like the star of a fairy tale as my dress would flare out like a blooming flower. It always ended in a delightful dizziness, absolute joy in being alive, and some giggles. Now, I always encourage my granddaughters, Sarah and Macy, to twirl. Is it even really a good day if you haven't twirled? It's such a magical reminder of being a child, being loved, and being known. It's also a reminder of being enough. All of which we are with our Heavenly Father. The Bible tells us that Jesus loved little children and invited them to be with Him (Matthew 19:13–15). This invitation still stands. Jesus invites us to be like children, not just any children, though, His children. Never forget you are a daughter of the King. You are His beloved. You are His child. He invites us, He welcomes us, and loves us. Mary understood that kind of childlike devotion. She wasn't concerned about appearances or performance. She simply wanted to be close to Jesus, sitting at His feet, completely at peace in His presence. That is indeed something to twirl about, and that is something to choose to stay connected to, even in December.

As our tea time together comes to a close, I'm curious what your big takeaway from our conversation will be. For me, it's the realization that we can receive Christmas instead of trying to produce it. Christmas is something we've been given. In fact, the greatest gift of Christmas was already handed to us on a holy night some 2,000 years ago when love was born. Jesus is the gift, freely given, no assembly required. And the joy I've worked so hard to have and spread can actually only be received from Him, just by being in His presence. So you see, the pressure's off because the most important part of Christmas isn't something we have to bake, buy, or build. Just like one of my favorite Christmas hymns, "Oh Little Town of Bethlehem", tells us, our role is to be like "meek souls and receive Him still." So let's not just welcome Jesus, but let's receive Him. Let's give of ourselves from the gifts He's already given us. Enjoy a Christmas that reflects who you are. Who God created you to be. Don't settle for a forced Instagram or Pinterest scene. Don't exhaust yourself chasing what is not necessary. Choose and keep what can't be taken from you. This will enable us to have the Christmas we've always longed for. I also think that this will give Christ the perfect birthday gift. The one He's always wanted. It's us. It's us worshiping Him with the gifts He has given us.

I'll miss our conversations, the quiet moments we've shared together with open hearts and steaming mugs. There's something special about sitting with a friend and struggling together. Someone else who understands the frustrations that Christmas can bring. Who understands the pull between doing and being, the tension between pressure and peace. We've laughed, reflected, sipped, and sorted through the season together. And I'm so grateful for every moment. When you write a book, you think about your reader. You imagine how you might journey together from one place to another, heart to heart, page by page. And now that I've walked this path with you, I can honestly say: it's touched my heart more than I ever expected. In hindsight, I'm so grateful the Lord gave me this opportunity. I realize now that He's been writing this message on my heart for quite some time. Maybe, in His sweet and surprising way, I've been His reader. That personal realization has made it possible for me to honestly journey with you. Not as someone with all the answers, but as someone who's walking it out right beside you.

And while I will miss our conversations, I'm excited and anxious to see what God has ahead for both of us this season. May we each stay near His heart, keep choosing the better part, and never forget that we were not meant to do this alone.

May this Christmas season be the one where peace doesn't just visit your home, but settles in your heart.

May you find joy in the quiet, strength in surrender, and deep rest in the presence of the One who came for you.

May your "yes" be wise, your pace be gentle, and your focus steady on the Savior.

And may you feel His love in the smallest moments, because that's often where it shines the brightest.

So warm up the kettle one last time, friend. Steep your soul in His presence.

And as you sip, remember that the best part isn't what's wrapped under your tree. The best part is the One who came wrapped in swaddling clothes. He came as a baby, He learned to walk, and He kept walking all the way to the cross for you and for me. Every step He took was for love, so that we could walk in grace, rest in peace, and live with a joy that carries us through every season, even Christmas.

I wish you that joy and a very Mary Christmas.

—Ann

Ponderings 

- Spend time in prayer, preparing wisely to say a strong yes to Jesus this Christmas, receiving the gift of the first Christmas, and also receiving Him again in your heart.

Grace

Remember when we first met? I was sitting in my car, with my festively dressed children, wedged against the wall. Yes, that wall, the one I had crashed into. The one that runs alongside our driveway. The incident was, of course, totally my husband's fault. Glad you're with me on that. Oh, and "Jingle Bells" was cheerfully blaring on the radio in the most annoying way possible.

Well, that wasn't just a "whoops" moment. That was the moment every ounce of pressure I'd been quietly stuffing down all season came bursting out like an overstuffed stocking. I know you well enough now to admit that quite a few colorful words escaped my mouth that day. Let's just say Clark Griswold would've nodded in admiration. And did I mention this was early December? Yep. That early. My holiday spirit didn't just slip away; it got totaled right there in the driveway. I knew our season was doomed before it even began.

So much has changed since then. I have changed since then. I know where my joy comes from now, and I'm learning to focus on that instead of all the pressure and demands swirling around me. But I can still totally relate to those blow-up moments during December, and I'm guessing you can too.

The good news? I think I could handle that moment differently now. Maybe even avoid it altogether. The tougher truth? There are still a million ways to get off track at Christmas with everything moving so fast and pulling at us from all sides. But the remarkable news? Not one of my kids even remembers this event. That honestly shocks me. But it also humbles me. Because there's so much grace in that. I'm so grateful for a Heavenly Father who loves us that tenderly. I'm also grateful for my wise husband, who's become pretty comfortable being under the bus.

Acknowledgements

Setting out on the unknown path of writing this book felt a bit like stepping into a fog with an old flashlight. But thankfully, I wasn't walking alone. Instead of a short-lived light source, I was following my Shepherd who had called me and was perfectly maneuvering all the boulders and sharp pebbles along my path. As John the Baptist might be paraphrased—'I indeed.....But He...' (Matthew 3:11)—when addressing the difference between how he baptized and how Jesus baptized, I repeat the phrase with this book. I indeed wrote the words on the pages, but He wrote them first on my heart. I have been blessed with some intimate moments with Jesus in my life, but this multiple-year yoked walk with Him has been really indescribable and must be acknowledged and marked. My hope for you is that when the Lord calls you to something way beyond your ability, you will say a strong yes and never look back as He perfectly, even if sometimes painfully, moves you forward.

This journey also required the help, prayers, patience, and love of many. Some actively jumped in with me, and others graciously released me for a while, understanding that I was called to this work for a season. This time turned out to be a long season, and I look forward to the reunions ahead, particularly with some dear friends who have bought a farm that I can't wait to visit. Life didn't pause for anyone as I wrote this book, and I'm aware of the heartbreak, grief, and unexpected turns some of my friends have faced. There have also been celebrations and new little humans to welcome. While I've prayed and been with you in spirit, I can't wait to actually be with each of you again. And to my faithful Mahjong girls, thank you for not revoking my seat at the table. Your friendship, patient "holds", and general good humor when I could play were a ministry all their own.

Now, for the people who were not blessed with supporting me from a distance but instead had to deal with me on a regular basis. As I repeatedly stumbled, each of you kept me going. First, Brian Dixon and hope*books. Brian, you gave me the courage and the actual method to be obedient to this calling. While the timing of your method and God's timing of my words didn't always match, you repeatedly honored my conviction to never get ahead of the Lord. Thank you for your patience, wisdom, and well-timed encouragement. Hope Dover, you are an incredible model of God's grace. Thank you for your patience with my endless and often repetitive questions. You explained the publishing process in a way I could understand and helped me with my very primitive computer skills to get every component of this book where it was supposed to be. Incredibly, you weren't doing this just for me, but for many aspiring authors, all while writing your own book at the same time. To the other editors and designers (particularly Lauren Scott) at hope*books, thank you for your commitment to my book and for honoring me with your talents. I know the Lord delights when you each use your gifts to get His word out!

I am blessed with wonderful praying friends. They are all over the world and have prayed diligently over this book and over me. The power and buoyancy this has given me is impossible to define or even really know, but it has been powerfully felt. This journey has been hard and filled with unexpected difficult times for my family. But through it all, the worldwide Sports Friends community has fasted, prayed, and supported me on every front. It's a strong and beautiful reminder of God's church and the loving bond we all share as brothers and sisters in Christ.

There are a few friends I particularly want to mention.

Marcy, from the very first time I very quietly, quickly, and humbly mentioned this "calling" while we stood on my front porch, you've been with me. While we have laughed and cried along the way, you never laughed at the undertaking of this project. My obedience was slow, but knowing that you were with me as a warrior in prayer meant so much. From the beginning and through the fiery arrows along the way, you have prayed faithfully. Thank you, dear friend.

Kim, first, a flat-out thank you for being a human Google for me and many others. Your writing and editing skills have been so helpful. I loved our "brainstorming" sessions, especially on our travel journeys. I could never write quickly enough to grab all the ideas you offered! Your support and encouragement when I wasn't hearing from the Lord were essential to my sanity as well as my momentum. Thank you, dear friend.

Beth, I don't think you realize what a rock you have been to me ever since you learned about this book. Helping me with access to talk with younger moms and getting their feedback was a tremendous boost. Your prayer support and wisdom have been a beautiful part of this story. And even personally providing me with an ideal opportunity to speak. Thank you, dear friend.

Anne, your encouragement throughout this journey has been a blessing. You always seemed to check in at the perfect time and offer just the right support. Your ideas on getting the books into the right hands and raising awareness of its existence have been so helpful. You pull me out into the world when I've been a writing hermit too long. And our quick retreat, well, it was just what the doctor would have ordered if consulted. Thank you, dear friend.

Okay, I've been putting off this next group because I'm at a loss for words. But it's time. These are my people. My family has both had to release me as I followed this call, and they have had to walk beside me for a journey much longer than any of us expected. My grands—Tripper, Sarah, Macy, and Davy—have had to deal with the fact that Nana's book has no pictures (although I did hide two things for them to find on the front cover). Then Tripper kept informing me that he had written five books in the time it was taking me to write one. I have missed some playtime when we're together, and while excited about it all, the whole book thing has sort of played out with them, and they are ready to get back to normal. I'm ready to join them! "Last one in the pool..."

Mom, little did we know that after I had my fall, you would have one too. Throughout your recovery, you have been so patient when I couldn't get there, and also put up with me writing when I was there. Quite a pair we are. Thank you for supporting me and encouraging me from the sidelines. It has meant so much.

Ashley, Bo, and Mac—once the initial shock of Mom writing a book had settled, you have each been totally supportive of this project. We've shared many Christmases together, and you three have definitely seen firsthand my deep desire to make everything just right, and probably noticed my exhaustion more than I imagined. I'm deeply thankful for your willingness to let me share some of our stories, and you, Mac, for understanding why I couldn't include everything you suggested. Bo, your calls checking in for updates were so thoughtful, encouraging, and always somehow perfectly timed. Thank you for that gift. Mac, your ideas and book cover designs kept me going and challenged me. I appreciate the interest you showed in this whole process. And to Mary Rachel and Sydney, who joined our family and brought along your own beautiful Christmas traditions. Thank you for eagerly embracing ours, too. You've each added so much richness to how we celebrate and brought space for joy into the chaos. The topics for this book were greatly influenced by discussions we have had together. To all of you— thank you for giving up plans, forgiving my absences, and generously offering both helpful ideas and listening ears when I needed to talk something out. I couldn't have done this without each one of you, and I wouldn't have wanted to. Thank you.

Ashley, you've been on this journey with me every single step of the way. Every step. Every need. When I needed encouragement, a break, or just a change of scenery, you listened when I needed to ramble through a spiritual thought at length. You've shown up with treats, candles, and author mugs to keep me moving forward and lighten the load. You've taken my frustrated calls in the midst of your own ministry work, even editing podcast recordings several times because I have interrupted with a mistimed urgent call. More than anything, though, thank you for showing me what it looks like to say "yes" when God calls. You've modeled the sacrifice and the blessing of obedience. Watching you live that out has been a great encouragement and a strong motivation for my "yes" to this book. Thank you, Ash.

And finally, Bob. The last and most important thank you belongs to you. And while there is so much to say, it is somehow the hardest to put into words. Partly because emotions and tears come, blurring my thoughts and my typing. But primarily because you have endured so much. You've accepted my absence with more patience than I deserve. You've grocery-shopped, cooked, run errands, and spent more quiet weekends alone than either of us cares to count. You've read and reread chapters, cheered me on when the words wouldn't come, and delivered chocolate when I needed it most. You too acknowledged my tea habit and brought author mugs to keep me going. You carried the weight of my broken wrist right alongside me, put up with stacks of paper everywhere, and survived way too many nights when dinner was, well, not even an option. One of my favorite expressions of your support, though, has to be the Christmas boxers you purposely wore throughout these months of writing. Perhaps all the Christmas music I had on repeat inspired a little extra festive spirit! Whatever it was, it was a happy reminder of your support and made me smile.

But more than all of this, you have covered me in prayer daily, hourly, and even in particularly hard moments, as we've walked this road together. You have seen the continual struggles and attacks and have suffered from them yourself. Yet we have once again experienced the Lord's faithfulness in these battles. Bob, there is no one I would rather journey with on my faith walk than you. Through the years, the Lord has given us some unbelievable opportunities as well as some unexpected twists and turns. I love how we've said yes and always jumped in faithfully together. When I said yes to this book, I knew you would be jumping in with me, and you have remained with me the whole way. I could have never written these pages without you being where you've always been and hopefully always will be, right beside me. Thank you for being such a steady rock for me. I love you. I love us.

Umm, about the "under the bus" thing....